" 'Because It Feels Good' Isn't The Best Reason For Doing Something,"

Abbie murmured.

"No? I happen to think it's a wonderful reason for doing something. One of the very best." As Dylan spoke, he reached out to sketch a brief line from the corner of her mouth to the underside of her jaw.

His work-roughened finger created havoc within Abigail. But the instant she realized she'd actually closed her eyes with pleasure, she snapped out of her Dylan-induced trance.

Stepping away from temptation, she said, "Trying to practice some Gypsy magic on me, too? If so, you can forget it," she added crossly. "Understand?"

Dear Reader,

The holidays are always a busy time of year, and this year is no exception! Our "banquet table" is chock-full of delectable stories by some of your favorite authors.

November is a time to come home again—and come back to the miniseries you love. Dixie Browning continues her TALL, DARK AND HANDSOME series with *Stryker's Wife*, which is Dixie's 60th book! This MAN OF THE MONTH is a reluctant bachelor you won't be able to resist! Fall in love with a footloose cowboy in *Cowboy Pride*, book five of Anne McAllister's CODE OF THE WEST series. Be enthralled by *Abbie and the Cowboy*—the conclusion to the THREE WEDDINGS AND A GIFT miniseries by Cathie Linz.

And what would the season be without HOLIDAY HONEYMOONS? You won't want to miss the second book in this cross-line continuity series by reader favorites Merline Lovelace and Carole Buck. This month, it's a delightful wedding mix-up with *Wrong Bride, Right Groom* by Merline Lovelace.

And that's not all! *In Roared Flint* is a secret baby tale by RITA Award winner Jan Hudson. And Pamela Ingrahm has created an adorable opposites-attract story in *The Bride Wore Tie-Dye*.

So, grab a book and give *yourself* a treat in the middle of all the holiday rushing. You'll be glad you did.

Happy reading!

Lucia Macro

Senior Editor
and the editors of Silhouette Desire

Please address questions and book requests to:
Silhouette Reader Service
U.S.: 3010 Walden Ave., P.O. Box 1325, Buffalo, NY 14269
Canadian: P.O. Box 609, Fort Erie, Ont. L2A 5X3

CATHIE LINZ
ABBIE AND THE COWBOY

SILHOUETTE *Desire*

Published by Silhouette Books

America's Publisher of Contemporary Romance

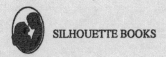

SILHOUETTE BOOKS

ISBN 0-373-76036-1

ABBIE AND THE COWBOY

CATHIE LINZ

left her career in a university law library to become a *USA Today* bestselling author of contemporary romances. She is the recipient of the highly coveted Storyteller of the Year Award given by *Romantic Times*, and was recently nominated for a Love and Laughter Career Achievement Award for the delightful humor in her books.

While Cathie often uses comic mishaps from her own trips as inspiration for her stories, she found the idea for this trilogy in her very own home—from an heirloom that has been in her family for generations. After traveling, Cathie is always glad to get back home to her family, her two cats, her trusty word processor and her hidden cache of Oreo cookies!

For everyone who still believes in magic!
With special thanks to my buddies,
especially Jean Newlin,
who helped me survive
The Summer of '95!

One

"**W**hoa!" Abigail Turner shouted, yanking on Wild Thing's reins as she tried to stop the bay mare from racing into the woods two hundred yards in front of them.

The horse kept going. And the woods kept getting closer and closer, each tree trunk looking like the dangerous barrier it would become if she were to collide with it. The branches were thick and full, creating an impenetrable fortress. There was no marked trail in that stand of trees; Abigail knew that much.

She also knew there was an extended family of prairie dogs located just before the woods, with the accompanying string of holes they burrowed into the ground—holes that could snap an unsuspecting horse's leg in two. If Abigail didn't get her runaway horse to swerve soon, she and Wild Thing might both be goners!

"Whoa!" The wind stung Abigail's eyes as she crouched low on Wild Thing's back to urgently repeat her command closer to the horse's ear. No luck.

Desperate now, Abigail tugged sharply on Wild Thing's reins, directing the horse to turn right. That didn't work, either. A good horsewoman, Abigail was bracing herself to stand in the stirrups and put all her body strength into halting the horse when she became aware of a thundering noise above the pounding of her heart and her own horse's hooves on the ground.

Out of the corner of her watering eyes, she saw a man riding hell-for-leather on a monstrous Appaloosa with spots as dark as the black Stetson the cowboy was wearing. "Let go of the reins!" he yelled at her. "And kick loose of the stirrups."

There was no time to argue. She did as she was told. A second later, the stranger had looped his arm around her and scooped her from her saddle to his, while both horses galloped side by side. The saddle horn banged against her thigh as he sat her across his lap, keeping her clamped against him with one hand while deftly handling his horse with the other. Wrapping her arms around his waist, she hung on for dear life.

In the transfer from her horse to his, the bandanna holding her hair in place had fallen off, loosening her long curly hair so that it blew into her face... and her unknown rescuer's face, as well. She couldn't see anything, and she didn't have a free hand to get her damn hair out of her eyes.

She felt him shifting, transferring the reins into the hand that had been pressed against her side. Seconds later, his horse, responding to the movement of his heels, veered right toward the open meadow.

It wasn't until they slowed down that Abigail got a view of Wild Thing, her reins in the man's capable sun-tanned hand as he led her. Abigail went limp with relief.

"Don't pass out on me now!" he growled in her ear.

She immediately stiffened again, on the defensive against the irritation she heard in his voice. Besides, now that the imminent danger was past, she was becoming all too aware of the way her denim-clad bottom was in such close proximity to a certain intimate part of his anatomy. She could feel every flex of the powerful muscles in his thighs as he urged his horse to a stop.

He kept Wild Thing's reins in his hand as the horse stood at a standstill behind them, her flanks heaving from exertion, her withers flecked with lather, but seemingly unhurt.

Tipping back his black Stetson with his right thumb, Abigail's unknown rescuer looked down at her. Shoving her hair out of her face, she tried to get her first good look at him. But his hat, although slightly angled, still created enough shadow that she couldn't tell much, except that he had devil-dark eyes.

"Mind telling me why you were riding like a maniac that way?" he inquired in a soft drawl that spoke of Western outlaws and desperados. It was gruff and dusty, silky and sexy all at once. Men didn't learn how to speak that way; they were born with the skill. She ought to know, since she was a successful Western-romance writer. Such men were her specialty—in fiction and in real life, she'd always had a weakness for cowboys.

But after three unsuccessful relationships, she'd recently sworn off getting involved with any more cowboys, vowing instead to keep them within the confines of her popular books. Things worked out better that way.

"I was *not* riding like a maniac," she belatedly denied. "My horse suddenly took off—"

"Listen, lady, maybe you better stay on a gentle mare until you have more riding experience—"

"I'm a good rider!"

"In an empty barn or horse stable maybe," he countered, "but not out here. It's just lucky for you that I came along when I did."

"Thank you," she said stiffly, in a starchy voice that her co-workers back at the Great Falls Public Library would have recognized as the one she reserved for troublesome patrons who wanted a book banned from the library. "You can let me go now."

"Not so fast," he replied, leaning back in the saddle to get a better look at her. "What are you doing out here all by yourself?"

"I could ask the same thing of you," she retorted. "This is private property." Seeing the direction of his wandering gaze, she put her hand to the open neckline of her shirt, wondering if he'd been able to see down the open V.

"Private property, huh?" he noted with a wicked grin that flashed across his face like summer lightning. "Meaning no trespassing?" he inquired, trailing one finger down her cheek to the curve of her jaw.

"Meaning that exactly," she haughtily returned.

"So what's your name?"

"What's yours?" she shot back.

"Dylan Janos, at your service, ma'am," he replied with another slight tip of his hat.

"Well, Mr. Janos, you can release me now. I want to see how my horse is doing. Something caused her to take off like a bat out of Hades...."

"Maybe she saw a snake or something."

"Wild Thing is too well trained to be spooked by a snake unless she was right on top of it, and she wasn't."

"Wild Thing?" Dylan repeated. "Whatever possessed you to ride a horse named Wild Thing? You'd do better on a nice nag named Muffin."

"She's *my* horse, and *I* named her Wild Thing," Abigail stated.

"You still haven't told me *your* name," he reminded her.

"That's right. And I don't intend to."

"Doesn't sound like you're being very friendly."

"Bingo," she retorted.

"You know, Gypsy legend has it that if you save a person's life, they owe you big-time. In fact, their very life belongs to you."

"Is that so? Well, Western legend has it that if you trespass on someone else's land, they have the right to..."

"Shoot me?" Dylan inquired dryly. "I do believe that's reserved for horse thieves, not trespassers."

She ignored his observation. "Western legend also dictates that a cowboy doesn't take advantage of a woman...."

"I haven't taken advantage of a thing. Not yet," he added, his flashing grin downright roguish this time.

"A gentleman would have let me go five minutes ago."

"I never claimed to be a gentleman."

"I can tell!" she declared, twisting suddenly to efficiently slide from his grasp and his saddle, landing on the ground on both feet with enough force to jar her back teeth.

Dylan dismounted a moment later. As he did so, she noticed the stiffness of his movement and the way he was rubbing his right thigh. She also noticed the way the denim of his jeans lovingly molded those masculine thighs before dismissing such things from her mind. Or trying to, anyway.

It was difficult, though. The man was six feet of rugged masculinity. At five foot eight, she was no shrimp herself. It wasn't until he moved closer that she realized he was limping slightly.

"Did you hurt yourself?" she asked in concern.

"You might say that," he replied darkly, his thoughts on the rodeo injury that had laid him up and forced him to retire from the rodeo circuit. The doctors had told him he'd been lucky to retain as much use of the leg as he had, lucky that he'd still been able to ride at all. But he'd never ride as he had before. The championship belt buckle he wore attested to his skill in the arena. A skill that had shattered along with the bones in his right leg. No, he wasn't feeling real lucky at the moment.

"Is there anything I can do?" Abigail asked.

"Yeah, you can tell me your name. And tell me what you're doing way out here. This is Pete Turner's ranch."

"That's right."

"And since I know Pete doesn't welcome visitors, I'd say you're the one trespassing, not me."

"How do you figure that?"

"Like I said, Pete doesn't care for visitors. He and I go way back."

"Really? Have you talked to him lately?"

"A few months ago. March, I think. February, maybe."

She knew all about cowboys and time. They lost track of it, the same way they lost track of money and women. It was now July.

Still, if Dylan had been a friend of her uncle's, she wanted to break the news of his death as gently as she could. While she struggled to find the proper words, he impatiently demanded, "Who are you?"

"I'm Pete's niece."

"No way! His niece is a starchy librarian in the big city."

Gritting her teeth, Abigail strove to ignore the *starchy* part of his description as she silently reflected on the ironic fact that both her chosen professions were rife with misconceptions. "I'm a librarian. Or at least I was until a few weeks ago."

Dylan eyed her from head to toe as if suspecting her of lying. "You don't look like any librarian I've ever seen," he replied.

"Really? And when was the last time you were inside a library?" she countered sweetly.

Dylan had visited the hospital library plenty while laid up, although he wasn't about to tell her that. He preferred to think about her, wondering what kind a librarian rode a horse called Wild Thing. One he wanted to get to know better, Dylan decided. She was all long legs and sleek curves. And her hair reminded him of curly ribbons of silk. It had caressed his face like a slender, seductive rope trying to lasso him and capture his heart—clinging to his rough skin with gentle abandon, rich with the scent of lily of the valley, his favorite flower.

Realizing that he was staring at her mouth without hearing a word she'd said, Dylan murmured, "What?"

"Never mind." Ignoring him, she ran her hands over Wild Thing's chest and withers, then her legs and hooves, even inside the horse's mouth, checking her for anything suspicious. Abigail's first search turned up nothing; the bay mare wasn't injured, thank heavens. The horse was still quivering slightly, but her limbs weren't swollen or cut. A more thorough search, after removing the saddle, provided the answer Abigail had been looking for. "I knew it!" she exclaimed. "I was set up!"

Two

___

"What are you talking about?" Dylan demanded.

"I *knew* Wild Thing wouldn't take off like that for no reason. Look at this!" She showed him the burrs attached to the saddle blanket. Sure enough, there were matching marks on the horse's flank, although her mahogany color made them difficult to see at first. "You poor baby," Abigail crooned, making Dylan wish she'd talk that way to him instead of her horse.

"Didn't you check your rig when you saddled her?" he asked.

"Of course I did. Those burrs weren't on that blanket then. It may have taken a while for them to work far enough under to really irritate her, but when they did, she bolted. And there's no way I could have picked up burrs in that location on the saddle blanket unless someone deliberately put it there."

"Did you leave the horse unattended after she was saddled?"

"Just for a minute. I got a phone call on my cellular phone...."

Dylan rolled his eyes.

"It was my editor from New York," she continued. "But I only stepped away for a few minutes, no longer than five."

"Long enough for someone to mess with this blanket," he said, reaching out to rub the mare's nose.

"Wild Thing doesn't like total strangers touching her," Abigail warned him.

"Like her owner that way, is she?" Dylan countered, soothing the skittish horse with his large hands, calmly reassuring her. The mare, darn her traitorous soul, ate up the extra attention.

Remembering the feel of that hand on her cheek, Abigail shivered. Dylan's fingertips had been work roughened. She didn't have to look at the palms of his hands to know they'd be callused and nicked. This was no city cowboy. He was the real thing.

"So why do you think someone would want you thrown from your horse?" Dylan turned to ask her.

"I don't know. Maybe because I refused to sell out to Hoss Redkins, the local bigwig bully."

"Sell out?" Dylan repeated with a frown. "You may be his niece, but this is still *Pete's* ranch and there's no way in God's green earth he'd sell to an overblown buffoon like Redkins."

Abigail bit her lip, realizing she still hadn't told him about her uncle's death. "My uncle passed away two months ago," she said quietly. "His attorney called me and told me he'd left the ranch to me."

"I thought he disowned his family when they sold out to Hoss."

"He did. Over the years, I tried to stay in touch."

"Yeah, I'm sure you did," Dylan retorted. "You'd want to stay in the good old guy's graces, after all."

"Meaning what?"

"Nothing," Dylan said wearily, taking off his hat and shoving his hand through his hair before setting the Stetson back on his head again. It shook him to realize that Pete was dead. Dylan had met him at a local rodeo where Pete had supplied some of the horses. The old man might have been about as friendly as a grizzly caught in a bear trap, but Dylan had enjoyed his company over the past ten years—since he'd moved west, in fact. Pete had taught him a lot. It pained him to think that Pete wouldn't be sharing any more tall tales of the "good old days" with him over a steaming cup of coffee generously laced with whiskey.

"So what are you going to do with the ranch now?" Dylan asked.

"Why, keep it, of course."

"Keep it? Like some kind of science project? Do you have any idea how much work it takes, not to mention money, to run a ranch, even one as small as this one?"

"I have a good idea, yes. I did a lot of research before I came up here."

"At the library down in Great Falls, no doubt," he said mockingly.

"That's right. And don't forget that I grew up on the ranch next door."

"Decades ago."

Stung, she said, "It wasn't that long ago!"

"Yeah? How old are you?"

"How old are *you*?" she retorted.

"Twenty-eight."

My God, he was just a baby! Well, maybe not, she amended, noting the fit of his jeans. He was definitely all grown-up. But he was a good four years younger than she was.

Thirty-two had never felt so old to her before, but then she'd never been attracted to a younger man before. She was also vastly irritated by him, she reminded herself, lest her hormones incite a temporary memory loss.

"Let me guess, a gentleman never asks a lady her age, right?" Dylan said. "So, Ms. Librarian, are you and your horse going to come along quietlike, or am I gonna have to lasso you?" Seeing her startled look, he continued, "I've got a double horse trailer parked a short ways away. It's attached to my pickup, and I can give you both a lift back to the ranch house."

"If you think I'm going to hitch a lift with a stranger—"

"I'm not the stranger, you are. You know my name. I still don't know yours."

"It's Abigail," she replied, staring him right in the eye, the tilt of her chin a challenge and a dare. "Abigail Turner."

"See, that wasn't so hard, now, was it?" he teased her, but she was no longer paying attention.

It suddenly occurred to her that maybe she was looking a gift horse, or in this case a gift *cowboy,* in the eye here. "Now that I think about it, you might be just what I'm looking for," she murmured.

"Really?" he murmured right back with a lift of one devilish eyebrow. "And how do you figure that?"

"Are you looking for a job?" she asked.

"Why? Are you aimin' on hiring me for something?"

"Maybe. I know you're experienced . . . with horses, I mean," Abigail added in a rush. She felt like an idiot. "I write better dialogue than this," she muttered.

"You do?" Dylan replied. "That mean you're a writer?"

"That's right." She lifted her chin, waiting for the inevitable question—*What do you write?*

Instead, he cautiously said, "What kind of job are we talking about here?"

"I don't suppose you take dictation, do you?" she couldn't resist inquiring with the slightest of smiles.

"You'd suppose right."

"How about typing?"

"Nope."

"Is that championship belt buckle you're wearing really yours?"

His dark eyes gleamed in the sunlight. "Want to check out the initials yourself?" he inquired wickedly, propping his two thumbs behind the wide silver buckle in a gesture that was downright inviting and very, very sexy.

For a moment, Abigail wondered what he'd do if she called his bluff. Then she decided she'd better not find out. At least, not right now. "I'm looking for a temporary ranch foreman," she said briskly. "During the past few years, my uncle wasn't able to keep up with things, and the property and fences show it. There's also livestock to be taken care of. I need someone willing to work hard. Hoss has put out the word, so none of the men around here will apply for the job. I should warn you that if Hoss scares you, then this isn't the job for you."

"Hoss doesn't scare me." *You do,* Dylan almost added. The blond librarian might be old Pete's niece, but she looked city bred and very high maintenance. Her jeans weren't anything fancy, nor was her denim shirt, but she had a way of carrying herself that was downright feminine. Yet she'd been quietly confident when she'd checked her horse, moving with quick capability. The woman was a study in contrasts. And she smelled like lily of the valley. Damn.

Her problems weren't his, he reminded himself. If he had a lick of sense, he'd remount and head on out. But cowboy chivalry demanded otherwise, just as it had decreed that he rescue her when he'd seen her wildly racing off across the meadow. Dylan wasn't the kind of man who went looking for trouble, but somehow trouble always seemed to find him anyway, despite the fact that he liked to keep moving.

His roving life-style suited him just fine; he wasn't looking to settle down. His older brother might have gotten married and his sister might have eloped, but Dylan wasn't ready to be put out to pasture just yet. Not by a long shot.

Still, Dylan never could resist a challenge, be it from a horse that they said couldn't be ridden or a woman as bristly as a porcupine. There was something about both that made his Gypsy blood run hot.

Wild Thing snorted and impatiently stamped her foot, as if publicly declaring her irritation with being ignored.

"I think I *will* take you up on that offer for a lift," Abigail decided. "Then we can talk some more about the foreman's job when we get to the ranch house."

Once the horses were safely ensconced in the double horse trailer and Abigail had climbed aboard the front bench seat of his pickup, she had the distinct feeling that she'd just taken the first step in an entirely new direction for her life. Only problem was that she wasn't sure this was the *right* direction.

Dylan wouldn't stay long; cowboys rarely did. But maybe he'd stay long enough for her to get someone more permanent for the job. Someone older and preferably married. Someone settled down.

Not that the words *settled* and *cowboy* often went together. They never had in her experience. Her third and final relationship with a cowboy had ended two months ago with him heading for Arizona and her nursing a broken heart. She'd be the first to admit that it was rather ironic that a successful writer of Western romances like herself could write a best-seller of a happy ending, but couldn't seem to find one for herself. At the moment, she was more concerned with finding out exactly who'd sabotaged her horse—putting both her and Wild Thing's safety, if not their very lives, in jeopardy.

"What the hell is that?" Dylan demanded, staring in disbelief at a strange-looking structure perched alongside the gravel lane heading to the ranch house. The compact building looked as if it had sprung from the earth and, unless his eyes deceived him, it even had grass on the roof. He knew Pete had been getting a little eccentric in his later years, but he wouldn't have built something this bizarre.

"That's Ziggy's place," Abigail replied as Dylan pulled his pickup truck to a slow halt.

"Who the hell is Ziggy?"

"A friend of mine."

"And you let him build that monstrosity on your land?"

"Ziggy is an artist."

As if to accentuate that point, the sudden and unmistakable roar of a power saw filled the air, causing a jay sitting on a nearby cottonwood branch to go skittering across the sky in raucous disapproval.

The sound of horses' hooves hitting the bottom of the horse trailer conveyed their nervous reaction to the unfamiliar loud noise.

"Get him to turn that damn thing off!" Dylan ordered her in a growl. "He's upsetting the horses."

"Wait a second, who's the boss around here?" she demanded, but she was speaking to empty air since Dylan had hopped out of the pickup cab and gone around back. By the time she'd slid out of the truck, Dylan was already marching over to Ziggy's place as if determined to shut him up himself.

Even though the day was sunny and warm, Ziggy was wearing his customary Swiss army cap. His shaggy white hair stuck out at wild angles from beneath it. Baggy overalls, a plaid lumberjack shirt and work boots completed his outfit. The middle-aged outdoorsman and wood-carver was described as unique by his friends, crazy by his enemies and talented by those who bought the sculptures he carved out of whole tree trunks. He was up to his ankles in sawdust and standing to one side of the weird dwelling he'd built.

Ziggy spoke English with an accent, but whenever he was upset he reverted to German and French curses mixed with a touch of Italian—a result of his Swiss heritage. When Dylan interrupted him, Ziggy glared and the international string of swear words filled the air instead of the sound of the power saw.

"How can I work when I am always interrupted?" Ziggy demanded of Abigail, his tone much aggrieved.

"*Baaaaaaaah.*"

"Now see what you are doing? You are upsetting Heidi und Gretel," Ziggy stated.

"Who are they? Your kids?" Dylan asked.

"In a matter of speaking," Abigail replied on Ziggy's behalf. "*Goat* kids," she added, pointing to the grass roof, where a trio of goats was munching on the grass.

To her surprise, the beginning of a rueful smile tugged at the corners of Dylan's lips, making her realize what perfectly sculpted lips they were. As before, the brim from his hat shadowed much of his face from her view, but the sun shone full force on his mouth, accentuating the aesthetic curve of his upper lip and the sensual fullness of the lower one.

"Nice friends you've got here," Dylan drawled.

"No *kid*ding," she replied with a grin of her own.

He groaned. "You didn't say anything about bad puns being part of this job."

"That bother you?" she inquired saucily.

"Do I look bothered?" he countered. Using the tip of his thumb, he angled his hat a little farther back on his head. The shape of the broad brim gave an added edge to his appearance. Aside from a red cardinal's feather, there was nothing fancy about the rather dusty black Stetson, and there was nothing fancy about Dylan. She had a feeling that the L-shaped rip in the left leg of his jeans wasn't a fashion statement, but was instead a sign of wear and tear.

Feeling her eyes on him, Dylan decided that turnabout was fair play. So he stared at her, his gaze appreciative and speculative, as he fantasized that he was touching her with more than just his eyes.

"Stop that, you two!" Ziggy commanded. "I can feel fire from here. All this emoting is too distracting for an artist like me."

Dylan watched the pink blossom in Abigail's cheeks and shook his head in amazement. "I thought blushing was a lost art," he murmured.

"It's sunburn," she shot back. "We're leaving now, Ziggy."

"My name's Dylan, by the way," Dylan said, nodding at Ziggy by way of introduction. "You been working on this piece long?" he added, indicating the tree trunk Ziggy had been carving.

"Since early this morning," Ziggy replied.

"Did you happen to see Abbie here go riding by while you were working?"

"My name is Abigail," she inserted.

"*I* call you Abbie," Ziggy commented.

"That's because you're my friend. Dylan is..."

"The new ranch foreman," he said on his own behalf. "Temporarily."

"You will be helping Abbie, then," Ziggy noted with a wide smile. "That is good. She needs help. I can do some but not everything. I am good with horses, I was raised on a farm near the Jura Mountains. We had horses and many cows. Goats, too."

"You're good with horses?" Dylan asked.

Ziggy nodded but added, "I'm better artist than cowboy."

"That's okay, Dylan here is the cowboy," Abigail said.

"Did you happen to visit the barn this morning?" Dylan asked Ziggy.

"I was here working on my sculpture all morning," Ziggy stated.

"Yeah, well, horses don't like loud noises, especially sudden ones. If you were raised on a farm, you should know that."

"Swiss horses are much better behaved than American ones," Ziggy maintained.

"Right. And I'm Buffalo Bill Cody," Dylan scoffed. "Just watch out when you use the saw, make sure that you don't make that racket when someone is riding nearby."

"No one rides nearby here," Ziggy declared. "They know I am working."

"Dylan, I really do have to get back to the ranch house," Abigail inserted, practically tapping her boot in impatience.

Once they were back on the road again and the sound of Ziggy's power saw was a distant annoyance, Abigail began questioning Dylan. "Why were you interrogating Ziggy that way?"

"Just trying to get a lay for the land. Did you see Ziggy in the barn this morning when you were saddling your horse?"

"Of course not. He likes horses but he loves sculpting. It's hard to drag him away from his work. Why the sudden curiosity?"

"Because someone put those burrs on your horse's saddle blanket."

"It wasn't Ziggy."

"What made you bring an eccentric like him up here?"

"He used to come into the library a lot. We'd talk about books and artists. Over the years, he became a friend. When I moved up here, I took pity on his neighbors in Great Falls, who were forever calling the authorities on him for using his saw at seven in the morning. I figured there would be enough space here on the ranch for him to be able to work in peace and quiet."

"I have a feeling peace and quiet don't go hand in hand with Ziggy."

"How about you? Does peace and quiet go hand in hand with you?"

"Sometimes."

"When you're sleeping, right?"

The image of her curled up asleep filled his mind, stealing into his soul. Did she sleep on her side or her back? And what did she wear to bed—a slinky nightgown, a cotton sleep shirt or maybe nothing at all?

"I usually make it a point to avoid trouble," Dylan said, as much as a reminder to himself as a reply to her.

"And how do you manage that?"

"By moving around a lot."

It was the answer she expected but not the one she wanted.

Coming around the corner of the barn and seeing the ranch for the first time never failed to touch Abigail's heart. Others might notice the weather-beaten smallness of the three-bedroom log house. They might see the work that needed to be done: the sagging gutters, the neglected yard, the slightly off kilter chimney. Even the porch swing hung unevenly and needed a new coat of paint.

But Abigail saw home. She had always loved the location of her uncle's ranch, which had an even better view of the surrounding mountains than her parents' ranch had had. A hillside rose directly behind it, with two tall fir trees standing sentinel atop it. In the evening, she'd climb the path up the hill and sit there, smelling the evergreen mixed with wood smoke from the cabin. Lower down, the aspens' pale bark glowed in the sunshine. The hill protected the house from the fierce northern winds, while the front porch had a southern exposure.

She and Dylan had unsaddled their horses without any further comment. Dylan had been as familiar with the layout of the barn as she was. And she'd discovered that his horse, an Appaloosa gelding, was aptly named Traveler.

Her thoughts of Dylan and his traveling ways were interrupted by the realization that they had company. An oversize man sat on his much besieged horse, glaring at Abigail's friend, Raj. The young woman was glaring right back.

"What are you doing here, Mr. Redkins?" Abigail inquired.

"Like I was telling your servant there—"

"Raj is my friend, not my servant," Abigail declared.

"Whatever. I'm here to see if you've decided to accept my offer to take this place off your hands," Hoss said, shifting in his saddle.

"And I told you that I'm not interested in selling," Abigail stated.

"I thought you might have changed your mind."

"Now, why would you think that?" Abigail demanded.

"Yeah, why would you think that?" Dylan drawled, speaking for the first time.

Instead of answering, Hoss said, "What are you doing here, boy? I heard you busted your leg in some rodeo down in Oklahoma. Come to loaf the summer off old man Turner, have you? Must have been a surprise to hear he'd kicked the bucket."

"Still as charming as ever, I see, Redkins," Dylan retorted.

"Is this man bothering you?" Hoss demanded of Abigail, his face florid as he glared at Dylan.

"No, but you are," she muttered under her breath.

"What was that?" Hoss asked.

"I said that Dylan is not bothering me. He's . . ."

"Come to help her," Dylan inserted.

"Hah!" Hoss scoffed. "You've come to mooch off a helpless woman, more likely. Dylan here has a reputation where ladies are concerned," Hoss informed Abigail. "He's got a string of buckle bunnies from Oklahoma City to Calgary. 'Course that was before he busted his leg."

The feel of Abigail's hand on Dylan's arm stopped him from hauling Hoss off his horse and stuffing his head in the nearest pile of horse manure.

"Dylan is a friend of my uncle's and he's welcome here," Abigail emphatically stated.

"I've just signed on as the ranch foreman," Dylan added for Hoss's benefit.

Hoss frowned at this news. "Why would you want to do that? I've never known you to stick around in one place very long. A job like this doesn't sound like something you'd want to get involved with."

It was one thing for Dylan not to want this job, but it was something else entirely for Hoss to try to tell him the job wasn't for him. No one told Dylan how to live his life, and he didn't tell others how to live theirs.

"What do you know about running a ranch?" Hoss was now demanding of Abigail. "Why, I heard you write them trashy romance novels—"

"You heard wrong," Abigail angrily interrupted. "I write *damn good* historical romance novels! There's nothing *trashy* about them! Unfortunately, I can't say the same about my neighbors," she said with a pointed look in Hoss's direction.

Much affronted, Hoss declared, "I don't write trashy romance novels!"

Abigail sighed. Her verbal insult had clearly sailed right over the man's ten-gallon-size head.

"Why don't you head on home, Redkins, now that you've dazzled Ms. Turner here with your charm and intellect."

"Why don't you mind your own damn business?" Hoss retorted. "What's it to you how long I chat with the lady here?"

"The lady here has asked you to leave her property," Dylan reminded Hoss, his eyes taking on a dangerous glitter.

"And what you gonna do if I don't leave?" Hoss taunted him. "You gonna throw me off with that busted leg of yours?"

"Don't tempt me," Dylan replied, his voice all the more dangerous for its softness.

"You and what army?"

"That does it...." Dylan growled, shaking off Abigail's arm and heading straight for Hoss with murder in his eyes.

Three

Fearing the worst, Abigail exclaimed, "Dylan, don't!"

But it was already too late. She watched with disbelieving eyes as—seemingly at Dylan's silent command—Hoss's horse suddenly reared, dumping the portly rancher smack in the middle of the water-filled rain barrel.

The resultant splash of water should have doused Dylan. Instead, it somehow miraculously missed him by a few inches.

His florid face bobbing like a red apple, Hoss sputtered, "H-how'd you . . . do that?"

"Me? I didn't do anything," Dylan denied with a lift of his eyebrow.

"I heard stories about you and that cursed Gypsy magic you practice," Hoss declared, eying him with equal parts of anger and suspicion.

"Hey, it's not my fault if you can't keep your seat, Redkins. You need any help getting out of that rain barrel?" he inquired with mocking courtesy.

"Keep away from me," Hoss yelled, making his horse sidestep even farther away. Hauling himself upright, Hoss added, "You're going to regret this, boy."

"I doubt it."

"Yeah, well, you just better watch your back," Hoss said, plunking his hat on his head—only to dump a ten-gallon-hat's worth of water on his head.

Abigail couldn't help herself. She cracked up, the laughter slipping out as she joined Dylan, whose grin was downright devilish, in his enjoyment of the moment.

Wiping the water out of his eyes before glaring at them both, Hoss said, "You're *both* going to regret this day."

"I don't think so," Dylan replied as a dripping-wet Hoss remounted his still-skittish horse.

Abigail could practically see the poor animal groaning under the rotund rancher's weight.

Watching the furious set of his thick shoulders as Hoss rode off, Abigail sobered as reality returned.

"That probably wasn't the brightest thing to do," she murmured.

"Who cares?" Dylan replied. "It felt damn good."

"That's no reason for doing something."

"No? I happen to think it's a wonderful reason for doing something. One of the very best." As Dylan spoke, he reached out to sketch a brief line from the corner of her mouth to the underside of her jaw.

His work-roughened finger created havoc within Abigail. She, who was supposedly fluent in the language of love after having written about it for so many years, found herself unable to describe this suddenly shameless surge of emotion. Instead, all she could do was give in to it, surrendering to the moment, even if only for a second or two. But the instant she realized she'd actually closed her eyes with pleasure, she snapped out of her Dylan-induced trance.

Stepping away from temptation, she said, "Trying to practice some Gypsy magic on me, too? If so, you can forget it," she added crossly. "Understand?"

"Sure do," he said in a clipped voice, anger tightening the skin on his lean cheeks and compressing his lips into a grim line. "I'm the hired help, and that's all. Since I don't exactly have folks lining up to hire me, I'd better be on my best behavior because, after all, there's not much need for busted-up Gypsy rodeo riders, right?"

"I didn't say that."

"Not in so many words maybe." His jaw clenched as he continued in the same hard inflection, "Listen, lady, there are plenty of other ranches I could be working at."

"I realize that."

"I don't need to go looking for trouble."

"If you want to leave, just say the word."

"Right," he scoffed. "And have you run Pete's ranch into the ground so that Redkins can get his greedy hands on the place after all? No way! I owe it to Pete to protect this place."

Dylan and Abigail were almost nose to nose, her blue eyes glaring into his dark ones, when the sound of Raj's voice interrupted them.

"Hey, I hate to interrupt such a friendly discussion and all, but I just wanted to know...is he staying for dinner?" Raj inquired. Her midnight black hair swung into a short page-boy cut just above her jawline, and her chestnut eyes gleamed with interest.

"Yes," Abigail said, taking a step back from the fire in Dylan's dark eyes.

"I'll add another place for dinner, then. By the way, my name is Raj Patel," she told Dylan.

"Pleased to meet you," he said with a polite nod of his head.

"And would you be Dylan Janos, by any chance?" she asked.

"That's right."

"How did you know his last name?" Abigail asked Raj.

"Because he's famous. Everyone knows who Dylan is."

Who I *was,* Dylan thought to himself, rubbing his thigh.

"Why, he was the best saddle-bronc rider in the NFR— National Finals Rodeo—championships in Las Vegas last year!" Dismissing Abigail's blank look, Raj explained to Dylan, "Abbie never reads the *ProRodeo Sports News.* I'm sorry she doesn't know how impressive your credentials are. Only the top fifteen cowboys in each event make it to the NFR," Raj told Abigail before frowning. "Dylan, I heard you'd been badly hurt...four months ago, was it?"

"Something like that." His voice was completely devoid of expression.

While his face was equally impassive, Abigail saw the briefest flash of something, an inner torment that compelled her to intervene. "I don't think Dylan wants to talk about it, Raj."

"I'm sorry," she said contritely. "Sometimes my enthusiasm gets ahead of me. Come on in and take a load off."

"I'd like to get settled in and clean up first," Dylan said. "If you'll just tell me where my quarters are."

"I'll show you," Abigail stated.

Once Dylan set his belongings down inside the small cabin set aside for the foreman's use, Abigail realized how little he had with him. She knew cowboys traveled light, and Dylan was no exception. She was willing to bet that most of the stuff in his gear bag was rigging related to riding.

He dwarfed the one-room cabin. He didn't have the muscle-bound looks of some of the men who graced the covers of her books. Instead, he was very lean and whipcord strong. She still remembered the powerful feel of his arms whisking her off her runaway horse a few hours earlier. She'd felt perfectly safe in his arms, yet she'd also felt a wild excitement that was at definite odds with the first emotion.

Clearing her throat, Abigail said, "Um, the bathroom is in the corner, and over here by the sink is a hot plate. It's not real fancy."

"I've stayed in worse."

"Yes, well..." Abigail paused to lean over and nervously smooth the quilt covering the bed. "You haven't tried the mattress from hell yet. Although I've never slept on it, when I aired the mattress I could *see* the lumps never mind feel them." She was babbling, but having Dylan and a bed in the same room definitely made her breathless. "Come on over to the house whenever you're ready. Supper is at six," she gulped before making her escape.

"Where's the fire?" Raj asked as Abigail came rushing into the kitchen.

"No fire. I just came to see if you needed some help," Abigail maintained.

"You mean you're not out of breath because of Dylan Janos? Now, *that's* hero material," Raj dreamily declared, tilting her head in the direction of the foreman's cabin.

Abigail shrugged nonchalantly. "He's just a guy."

"A darn good-looking one."

"His hair is too long."

"Hah!" Raj said triumphantly. "You're tempted."

"I am not!" Abigail denied.

Raj gave her a look that said she knew better.

"Okay, I might have been tempted at first," Abigail allowed. "In the very beginning, when he saved me. For a minute or two."

"Wait a second!" Raj squealed. "This is the first I've heard about him saving you. From what?"

"Boredom," Abigail retorted.

"Yeah, right. You've never been bored a minute in your entire life. Now, come on, tell me everything!"

"You know I took Wild Thing for a run this morning? Well, we hadn't been out long when she suddenly took off, and I couldn't stop her. She was heading right for that stand of woods in the north pasture, the one with the prairie-dog holes. Anyway, Dylan showed up out of no place and helped out."

"Helped out how?" Raj asked. "Anything that required you to end up in his arms?" Seeing the blush on Abigail's face, she crowed, "Aha! I knew it."

"I told you, I might have been tempted, but I got over it. Real fast. He's a cowboy."

"Yeah, I noticed," Raj said dreamily.

"Cut that out. He's working here. I'm his employer. And I am not about to repeat my past mistakes. You know my rule—no more cowboys. I've sworn off of them for good."

"You know what Katharine Hepburn said—'If you obey all the rules . . . you miss all the fun.'"

"I have all the fun I can manage at the moment, thank you very much," Abigail retorted tartly. "Besides, you're hardly an objective observer in all this. You're practically as bad about cowboys as I am."

"Nonsense. I am merely a fan of Western U.S. social life and customs."

"Yeah, right. That's putting it mildly. You think John Wayne walked on water and you got your master's degree in Western culture by writing a thesis on the cowboy as mythical hero."

"Not the most practical thing I've ever done," Raj admitted. "But then I'm not one to conform to expectations."

Raj had left her native India at the tender age of fifteen, to visit a third cousin who owned a restaurant in New York City. That had been twenty years ago, and she'd often told Abigail that she'd never looked back. By the time Abigail had met her in Great Falls, Raj was working as a waitress by night and taking college courses by day.

The first time Abigail had visited Raj's tiny studio apartment, she'd been overwhelmed by the Western memorabilia—classic posters of John Wayne and Barbara Stanwyck Westerns covered the cracked plaster walls, while their movies on video filled the bookcases and overflowed onto the floor.

It was a love that Abigail shared. She was lucky to have been able to combine her two loves—books and Western life—into her second career as a Western-romance writer.

"Yes, well, a lot would say that I wasn't practical leaving my job at the library in Great Falls to come up here and live on this ranch. My parents especially," Abigail noted wryly. "They think I'm crazy, that this is some passing phase I'm going through, and they're praying that I'll 'come to my senses' is the way my father put it, and sell the place.''

''To that idiot who was here earlier?''

Abigail nodded. ''My parents just don't understand, and I don't know how to explain it to them. The thing is that I feel such a sense of peace here, a sense of belonging. When I look at those mountains out there—'' she swept her hand toward the large window facing east ''—it just feels right in here.'' She pressed her clenched hand against her chest.

''Then you did right coming here.''

''Have I told you how much I appreciate you coming up here and spending the summer with me?'' Abigail said.

''Oh, yeah,'' Raj mockingly retorted, ''it was a *real* hardship for me to leave my cubbyhole apartment in Great Falls and spend two months in these gorgeous surroundings.''

''At least in Great Falls you didn't have to deal with moose on your doorstep.''

''That made our first morning here exciting, didn't it?'' Raj recalled with a grin. ''And I have a feeling that Dylan's presence is going to make the rest of our summer rather exciting, as well.''

''He's a little less homely than that moose was,'' Abigail replied with a saucy grin. ''But I'd be surprised if he stays the entire summer. His kind doesn't tend to stay in one place very long.''

''He might surprise you.''

''You can count on it,'' Dylan stated from the doorway.

Abigail swung around, her face turning red as she wondered how much of their conversation he'd overheard.

She found out when he mockingly added, "And I'm deeply honored that you think I'm less homely than a moose."

To her relief, Abigail was saved from having to make a reply by the noisy entrance of Shem Buskirk and his two grown sons, Hondo and Randy. Shem had worked on her father's ranch a few summers when she'd been a child. He'd been the only applicant Abigail had gotten in reply to an ad for help at the ranch. Considering the fact that Hoss owned the newspaper in the nearest town, Big Rock, she supposed she was lucky to have gotten her ad run at all. Hoss had told her that no one would answer it. He'd been wrong.

Not that Hoss considered Shem much of a threat. No one knew how old Shem actually was, but he told stories about his mining days in the Crazy Mountains in the early 1930s. He had a shock of white hair almost as wild as Ziggy's, while his face had more lines on it than a Manhattan road map. He'd turned down her offer of ranch foreman, claiming responsibility like that wasn't his strong suit, but had agreed to work for her.

His two sons—Hondo and Randy, as ageless as Shem—had just shown up with him. They were willing to work for room and board. The bunkhouse was empty anyway, so Abigail let them stay on. Neither one of them had what it took to be foreman.

The two "offspring," as Shem called his sons, reminded her of Mutt and Jeff, with Randy as tall and skinny as a rail while Hondo was much shorter and heavyset. Neither one was real bright, but they were adequate workers, although they didn't do anything without being told first. However, at this point, Abigail couldn't afford to be real choosy. Her uncle had let things go for the past few years, and there was plenty of work to be done.

Under cover of the noise Shem and his sons made whenever entering a room, Raj sidled up to Abigail to whisper, "I'm not sure how practical it was to hire Dylan when you've sworn off cowboys. It's kind of like putting a box of imported Belgian chocolates in front of a chocoholic who has just gone on a diet."

As always, Raj was right. It was one of her less endearing traits.

"Where's your yodeling friend tonight?" Hondo asked Abigail around a mouthful of mashed potatoes a few minutes later.

"Ziggy is working. Sometimes he comes over and takes over cooking duties from Raj," Abigail explained for Dylan's benefit. "You haven't lived until you've tasted his fondue."

The men all wore similar expressions of horror.

Abigail had to laugh. "Don't worry," she said mockingly. "I won't try and *force* you big, strong men to eat sissy food like fondue. Who knows what it might do to you?"

"You've got that right," Randy declared. "Food like that can affect a man's performance. Might make him—" he lowered his voice "—you know . . . competent."

"There's little chance of you ever being competent," Raj assured Randy.

"The word is *impotent*," Shem told his son. "You'd know that if you read the dictionary the way I do."

"I've got better things to do with my time than read a book that's better used as a doorstop," Randy retorted.

"Indubitably," Shem replied.

"Hey, are you calling me a name or something?"

"Look it up in your Funk and Wagnalls," Shem retorted.

"My what?"

"Never mind."

"Nice crew you've got here," Dylan mockingly murmured from her side. Trust Raj to seat him right next to Abigail.

Seen through his eyes, she didn't imagine Shem and his sons looked all that promising. Abigail was well aware that Dylan was only sticking around because he didn't think she was capable of hanging on to the ranch without his help. The damn thing was, he was right. Not because she wasn't capable enough, but because she did need help. His help. But she didn't have to be happy about it.

"Here, have some more peas," she said in a grumbly tone of voice, grabbing the bowl and shoving it in Dylan's direction.

She also wasn't happy about this jolt of sexual awareness from something as simple as his fingers brushing hers as he took the bowl from her. But she was a big girl, and she wasn't about to let something like chemistry control her. *She* was the one in control now.

Hondo wasn't as lucky, wrestling as he was with the yellow plastic container of mustard, turning it upside down and squeezing it as if trying to wring the last gasp of life from it. Hondo was the only person Abigail had ever met who put mustard on everything—including tonight's meal of meat loaf, mashed potatoes and peas.

"Works more expeditiously if you tilt it at an angle," Shem informed his son.

"Say what?"

"Better," Raj translated.

Hondo did as his father suggested, and sure enough the mustard finally came spurting out, along with the lid, spattering the tablecloth and poor Shem, who was sitting directly across from Hondo.

Aside from one pricelessly startled look, Shem's way of handling the situation was to simply keep on eating, as if he didn't have mustard dripping from his forehead and the bridge of his nose.

For the second time that day, Abigail lost control, laughing so hard tears came to her eyes and Dylan had to pat her on the back.

"I know the Himlicking maneuver if you're choking," Randy informed Abigail, which set her off again.

"What'd I say?" Randy asked in bewilderment.

"I need some air," Abigail gasped in between the tears of mirth.

"Right-oh," Randy said with a crack of his knuckles. "Step aside there, Dylan, and I'll give her the Himlicking."

"No, don't do that," Dylan said, somehow managing to keep a straight face. "I'll take her outside so she can get some air."

Once they were both outside, the cool night air and the closeness of Dylan by her side brought Abigail to her senses quickly enough.

Although it was nearly seven, the sun was still fairly high in the sky, nowhere near ready to set yet. This far north, sunset didn't come until after ten in June. Now it was July, and the days continued to be long and lovely. Abigail had always considered it Mother Nature's way of making up for the often brutal winters.

There was something about this time of year that had always given her a sense of peace, of hope. But that was before Dylan had ridden into her life. Now she felt restless and curious.

So she said, "When you helped me with Wild Thing earlier today, you said something about Gypsy legend—"

"When I saved your life, you mean?" Dylan interrupted her to say.

"Was that just a line?" she asked.

"About saving your life?"

"No, I meant about your having a Gypsy heritage."

His jaw tightened. "Does that matter?"

She sensed a certain defensiveness in his attitude. "I'm sorry. I wasn't trying to be nosy...."

"Sure you were."

"Okay, so I was," she amiably agreed. With a shrug, she added, "I'm a writer. I'm interested in people and their roots. Or aren't rolling stones like you allowed to have roots?"

"I've got roots. Back in Chicago with my family."

"You're from Chicago?"

Dylan grinned at the way she said the city's name, with the same sort of disdain used by most westerners to any city east of Denver. "I left home a long time ago. I'm the wanderer in my family. My dad says it's due to my Rom blood, Gypsy blood, which I got from him. Both my parents came over from Hungary in the early sixties, before I was born. My dad is Rom, my mom isn't."

"Are you an only child?"

"Nope, I've got an older brother and sister—Michael and Gaylynn."

"So you're the baby in the family. That figures," she murmured half under her breath.

"What figures?"

"The baby in the family is often spoiled with too much attention."

"You read that in some book? Or are you speaking from personal experience?"

"I'm an only child."

"Which means you were *definitely* spoiled."

"How do you figure that?"

"Maybe it's the way you walk around with your nose in the air."

"I do not!"

"Not that it's not a cute nose, mind. Just a mite haughty."

"If this is your awkward attempt to endear yourself to me..."

"Why would I want to do that?"

"It seems to go with the territory," she muttered darkly.

"And what territory might that be?"

"Cowboy territory."

"And I suppose you know all about cowboys?"

"I could write the book on them. In fact, I have written several of them. So trust me, I know all about cowboys with itchy feet," she loftily informed him.

"My feet aren't what's itching at the moment," Dylan lazily assured her. "It's something much higher up on my...anatomy."

"I have no wish to discuss your anatomy."

"You'd rather just look at it."

"That's right. I mean, of course not!"

"So you *would* rather talk about it."

"I'd rather ignore it."

"So would I. But that's hard to do, no pun intended, when I have this fierce ache..."

"I don't want to hear about it!"

"Right here..." His hand hovered suggestively before landing on his thigh.

"Maybe you should put some horse liniment on it," she suggested tartly. "I hear it works real well on stubborn mules, as well."

With that, she turned on her heel and marched back inside, leaving Dylan staring after her.

"First I'm cuter than a moose and now I'm a stubborn mule. I think she likes me," Dylan informed the orange barn cat curled up on the crooked front-porch swing. "I think she likes me a lot!"

Dylan's first week at the ranch flew by. Working from dawn until dusk when daylight lasted for over fifteen hours would do that to a man, make time fly by. But working for a woman like Abigail Turner did *other* things to a man, like turning his head. She'd done that, all right—with her wild curls that she constantly battled to keep out of her eyes, eyes as blue as the big Montana sky.

While standing under a spray of cold water from the shower, Dylan sang the opening lines of a George Strait classic. Cold showers had become a daily ritual for him since meeting up with Abbie. After getting dressed, Dylan grabbed a bottle of juice out of the tiny fridge and drank it straight from the bottle, all the while wondering what Abbie was doing this morning.

Dylan always thought of her as Abbie, even during those times when she stuck her adorable nose in the air and went all haughty on him. He'd never really had to chase after a woman before; usually they seemed to swarm around like bees to honey. Dylan was cynical enough to suspect that the buckle bunnies who followed the rodeo trail had found his championship buckle as appealing as he was. He'd noticed there sure as hell hadn't been any groupies hanging around the hospital when he'd been released.

Wiping his mouth with the back of his hand, he replaced the juice bottle and cooked up a mean Mexican omelet.

Dylan had just finished eating when he heard someone banging on his front door. It was Shem.

"Did you hear that strange noise?" the older man demanded. "It's stopped now, but it sounded kinda like a cross between a hyena and the howl of a mad dog. Randy claims he heard something that sounded like George Strait lyrics, but I told him no human being could sound like that."

Dylan wasn't about to admit that he was the culprit. It wasn't the first time he'd had this kind of reaction to his singing. Grown men had been known to crumple and beg for mercy when he let loose. Instead, he muttered, "I didn't hear a thing. Was that why you stopped by?"

"That and mail call. Got a package here for you. Thought I'd drop it off before heading on out." Without further ado, Shem shoved the package at him and took off.

The cardboard was dented and dinged, as if it had been shunted from pillar to post. Looking at the address label, he realized that indeed the package had made the rounds—starting with down in Arizona and following him three states north at his various forwarding addresses until reaching him here. The return address was almost illegible after all the official-looking postal stamps marked on it, but further study told him that it was from his sister, Gaylynn. The postmark was late May, nearly two months ago, and was listed as Lonesome Gap, North Carolina.

When he'd phoned his mother for her birthday a few weeks back, she'd told him that Gaylynn had gone and married Hunter Davis down in the Blue Ridge Mountains. The last time Dylan had seen Gaylynn had been April, at their older brother Michael's wedding to Brett. And now Gaylynn was married, too.

Dylan shook his head, hoping this matrimony bug wasn't contagious somehow. Not that marriage had been in his short-term plans before the accident, but now it was even further off. First he had to see how his recovery went this summer. He had orders to return to the doctor in Arizona come September for another evaluation. If the truth be known, Dylan still had this fantasy that he'd be able to return to the rodeo circuit. Reality dictated otherwise, but it was just so damn hard for him to accept that he'd *never* return to the life he'd loved for more years than he could remember.

Returning his attention to the package, he opened it up, thinking that he really should send Gaylynn and Hunter a wedding gift, even if they had eloped. His sister had looked and acted pretty skittish the last time he'd seen her, unusual for her since she was the fearless one in the family. But maybe that was because he'd seen her at Michael's wedding and reception, neither one of which had been a quiet affair—not with dozens and dozens of Janos cousins attending. His family was not known for their subdued natures.

Which was why Dylan hadn't told them about him being in the hospital. They would only have gotten hysterical and flown down to Arizona on the next plane. He'd had enough to cope with.

Despite the battering the package had taken en route, Gaylynn had packed the contents well, with plenty of those irritating plastic peanuts that stuck to your fingers like glue.

He found the note first.

Dear Baby Brother,

Hope this reaches you in good shape. I've enclosed the paperwork on this surprise for you, from the original note from our great-aunt Magda in Hungary, to the Post-it note Michael wrote me. I hope the box serves you as well as it has Michael and me. And listen, I think there's a side effect of this whole thing—I don't know how to explain it other than saying a new skill is bestowed upon the owner. For me, it was drawing—remember how I could never even draw a straight line before? I'll have you know that I've even sold several of my sketches now! Who'd have thunk it, huh?

Enjoy, Gaylynn

P.S. It's very old so take good care of it! Don't go tossing it into that sorry excuse of a bag you call a suitcase.

P.P.S. How about giving me a call sometime? They do have phones in Arizona, right? You heard I'm a married woman now? You remember how I had a crush on Hunter when I was thirteen? I almost gave you a black eye for saying that, so I figured you'd remember. The folks aren't happy that we eloped, but they are glad I resigned from the Chicago public-school system. Now I'm working at the Lonesome Gap Lending Library and very involved with bringing new life to this delightfully quirky town.

Attached to his sister's stationery was a crumpled Post-it note from Michael to Gaylynn. Dylan's older brother was much more laconic than his sister was, and his note was correspondingly brief.

Thought you might find this interesting. Brett swears it worked in our case. Judge for yourself.

And last of all was a letter in an unfamiliar spidery handwriting.

Oldest Janos son,
It is time for you to know the secret of our family and *bahtali*—this is magic that is good. But powerful. I am sending to you this box telling you for the legend. I am getting old and have no time or language for story's beginning, you must speak to parents for such. But know only this charmed box has powerful Rom magic to find love *where you look for it.* Use carefully and you will have much happiness. Use unwell and you will have trouble.

Reaching into the package one more time, Dylan found a tissue-paper-wrapped item. When he finally unwrapped it, he discovered an intricately engraved metal box. So this was the famous box—the one involving an out-of-whack love charm and a no-account count, as his sister had put it at the time.

Dylan had heard about it when he'd gone home for Michael's wedding. This little box had supposedly brought him and his new bride, Brett, together. And now Gaylynn thought it had done the same for her and Hunter.

Dylan just shook his head. His brother and sister had always been more fanciful than he was. He'd never heard if there was anything inside the box, though. All he'd heard was that after opening it, you fell in love with the first person of the opposite sex you looked at—if you believed that kind of thing, which he didn't. Shaking the box, he heard something hard clinking inside. Come to think of it, the box was kind of heavy for something so compact.

Opening it up, he found out why—inside was a flat geode the likes of which he'd never seen before.

A sudden shrieking scream jarred his attention from the geode and the Gypsy box to the front window, where he saw Abbie. She had her back to him and she appeared to be clutching the top rung of the corral's log fence. Her next shriek turned into a wail as she lost her footing and slipped, landing smack dab in the middle of a Montana-sized mud puddle.

Four

For a second or two, the Gypsy box seemed to hum in Dylan's hands before he abruptly set it down, all his attention now focused on Abbie, who had yet to get up. Had she hurt herself when she'd fallen? It wasn't that far from the top rung to the ground, but all you had to do was fall the wrong way...hell, he'd seen it happen enough times on the circuit.

Almost yanking the sagging cabin door off its hinges, Dylan rushed outside to check on Abbie. He came up from behind her, hunkering down to her side so he could see her face.

"Are you okay?" he demanded. "Did you hurt yourself? Is anything broken?"

"Just my image. Only a greenhorn falls off a corral fence," Abigail noted in rueful disgust. Seeing his concerned expression, she reassured him, "I'm not hurt, just embarrassed."

"Then why the hell didn't you get up?"

"Well, since I'm down here, I decided I might as well enjoy the luxury of the moment," Abigail replied with dry humor before adding, "You know, some women pay good money for a mud bath. Supposed to do wonders for the skin."

Dylan just shook his head as he held out a hand to help Abbie stand up. She never reacted the way he thought she would. Just when he thought he had her figured out, she threw him a curve. She had plenty of curves, from her silky hair to her lush breasts.

"Here, let me help you up," he said.

She shook her head, the wild waves of her golden hair bouncing around her slightly mud-spattered face. "That's okay, I can do it myself."

What she did herself was slip again, her supporting hand shooting out from under her and almost sending her facedown in the mud.

Dylan said, "Unless you're planning on making that a mud face mask, too, I'd suggest you take my hand."

"All right. Just don't try any funny stuff," she warned him before cautiously holding her hand out to him.

"Trust me, you look funny enough for both of us," he drawled, twining his fingers through hers as he helped her up.

"I'm getting you all muddy," she noted remorsefully, trying to disentangle her fingers from his before she got him even messier.

"It wouldn't be the first time," he murmured. "I've been dumped in my share of mud holes."

"Really? And here I was thinking you were such a hit with the ladies," she saucily stated.

"Very clever. You've got mud on your nose." When she instinctively raised her hand to wipe it away, he said, "No, don't do that. You'll just make it worse."

Looking down at her mud-spattered jeans, she ruefully replied, "I don't think that's possible."

"Anything is possible," he whispered before lowering his head to brush his lips across hers. Having expected a more forceful approach from him, she was charmed by his gentleness.

He cupped her elbows in his lean hands, but made no attempt to tug her into his arms. He didn't need to; his kiss was powerful enough to keep her close as he let his mouth do the convincing. The promise of more to come was there as he shifted his mouth and coaxed her lips to part, transforming the sweet kiss into a heated celebration of hunger and desire.

Abigail wanted him with a sudden fierceness that shocked her. Common sense was swept aside as certainly as his tongue swept across the delicately curved roof of her mouth. Her tongue darted to meet his with joyful eagerness. She hung on to the belt loops of his jeans as the world spun out of control all around her. With every breath she took, her breasts brushed against his chest, creating a waterfall of pleasure cascading throughout her entire body.

As if sensing her unsteadiness, Dylan slid one arm around her waist while shifting his other hand up to cup the back of her neck, enabling him to pull her more completely into his kiss, deepening it to another level of intensity.

Somehow she'd known with a feminine instinct that kissing Dylan would be dangerous to her peace of mind, but she hadn't had a clue that this kind of mindless bliss would be involved. This was alarming...so why wasn't she fighting? Why was she melting against him?

Because this felt too darn good to stop now.

She had no idea how long she would have stood at the edge of the horse corral—in plain view of the ranch house and the barn, kissing Dylan as if her life depended on it— had she not been interrupted by the unique blare of the horn on Ziggy's four-wheel-drive vehicle. It blared out the opening of *The Sound of Music*.

A rain barrel of cold water couldn't have brought her to her senses faster. Yanking herself out of Dylan's arms, she only then realized that she'd lifted her hands to his shoulders. Two muddy fingerprints left visible testimony to her actions.

To her relief, Ziggy was too caught up in his own news to say anything about the compromising situation he'd caught them in. "I finished my latest piece! It is brilliant! My best. I am brilliant! It talked to me. I was up all the night." Tugging her into his arms, Ziggy joyously kissed her cheek. "You have made a new man out of me, bringing me here to work. And to show my appreciation, I have come here. You are ready for bed now, yes?" Ziggy asked her.

"What kind of question is that?" Dylan growled, tugging her out of Ziggy's arms and right back into his.

"Don't be ridiculous!" Abigail snapped as she freed herself, angered by her own weakness where Dylan was concerned.

"You are having trouble here?" Ziggy asked, only now picking up on the sizzling sparks still flying between Dylan and Abigail.

Trouble couldn't begin to describe it, Abigail thought to herself. "Holy buffalo patties," she muttered under her breath.

Dylan blinked. "What did you say?"

"Abbie has her own special curses," Ziggy told him. "I can curse in three languages, German, French and Italian. I have offered to teach her some of these, but she prefers her own."

"What does that have to do with you asking her if she's ready for bed?" Dylan demanded, not willing to let go of that quite yet.

"Because I have finished bed for her." Ziggy pointed to the back of his four-wheel-drive vehicle, where Dylan could barely make out a rough-hewn wood headboard and footboard.

"Ziggy makes some wonderful pieces of custom furniture, as well as his sculptures," Abigail explained, releasing herself and moving a few feet away from Dylan.

"I also brought Mutti, Heidi and Gretel and put them in barn already. You said you could watch them while I am searching for more wood that talks to me."

"In German, French or Italian?" Dylan mockingly drawled before Abbie elbowed him in the stomach, adding another mud spot to his once-white T-shirt. Battle scars, Dylan thought to himself with a grin, and worth every twinge.

"Abbie, why are you full of mud?" Ziggy inquired.

"I slipped off the fence. Stupid thing for me to do, I've been sitting on fences just like that one since I was six years old. But all of a sudden, I just slid off." She shrugged. "I must be getting careless in my old age."

Dylan strolled over to test the top rail.

"What are you doing?" she asked him.

"Just making sure that it *was* an accident and not another incident of sabotage."

"You can't blame my own klutziness on Hoss Redkins. Unless you used Gypsy magic to toss me into a mud puddle the way you had that horse throw Hoss into the rain barrel.''

Magic? There *was* the charmed box, not that Dylan was about to tell her that. He was only too well aware of the suspicion with which his Rom background was viewed. While there were times it helped add to the mystique of his rodeo persona, there were also times when people checked their wallets after hearing about his heritage. The fact that he, born and raised in Chicago, had a supposedly magical way with horses only added to the image of him being different from the other cowboys.

Dylan didn't believe in breaking horses. He believed in converting them to his way of thinking. Good riding had more to do with your head than anything else, and your best tools were your hands.

He wondered if winning over Abbie was all that different. All he needed was a plan to woo her over, to convert her to his way of thinking.

He had to tune in to her reaction to his every move. With a horse, you checked its eyes and ears. Eyes were important with a woman, too, and Dylan had seen the conflict in Abbie's sky blue eyes. She'd wanted him. He'd tasted how much in the fiery kiss they'd shared.

Dylan had wanted women before, but never with this kind of bone-deep intensity. Abbie was like a thorn under his saddle, an itch that had to be scratched. He was determined to make her his. Sooner rather than later.

Opportunity knocked only seconds later when Ziggy asked for his help in carrying the heavy headboard and footboard upstairs to Abbie's bedroom.

Dylan immediately accepted while Abigail immediately protested. "Randy or Hondo can help you, Ziggy."

"They're out mending fences," Dylan said.

"Something you'd be wise to do," Abigail muttered with a warning glare.

"I'm just trying to be helpful, ma'am," he said with a lift of one devilish eyebrow.

The sight of Dylan in the inner sanctum of her bedroom proved to be as upsetting as she'd anticipated. For one thing, he looked much too at home for her peace of mind. And for another, setting up the new bed took entirely too long. Despite falling in the mud puddle, she didn't want to leave to go take a shower yet—the bathroom had a connecting door to her bedroom, and the idea of standing naked under a stream of water while Dylan stood on the other side of the door was just too tempting....

I meant too unsettling, she hurriedly corrected her thoughts, restlessly shifting her weight from one bare foot to another. She'd kicked off her boots in the mud room before coming upstairs. So had Dylan and Ziggy. Dylan had a hole in the right big toe of his white athletic socks, while Ziggy had red-and-green reindeer on his socks.

When she noticed Dylan glancing toward the pine bureau that Ziggy had made for her back in Great Falls, she realized that a corner of her pink cotton nightgown was cascading over the edge of the half-open drawer. Nonchalantly moseying over to the bureau, she shoved the nightgown and drawer back in place.

"I just won a bet," Dylan noted with a gleam in his dark Gypsy eyes. "I bet myself that you'd tidy that drawer within ten seconds of you noticing it."

"You notice entirely too much," Abigail retorted.

"Where you're concerned, there's no such thing as too much."

Abigail tried to come up with something smart and funny to say, but her mind was wiped clean, like a schoolroom blackboard being cleaned.

As if sensing her discomfiture, Dylan said, "I like the photograph of the aspens over your bed."

This she could make a sensible reply to. "Thanks. I took that picture in Colorado a few years back, but it reminds me of the aspen grove out back. Did you know that if you kill one aspen tree, the entire grove will die? That's why it's stupid to carve anything in the tree's bark."

"You mean like 'Dylan and Abbie' with a heart around it?" he inquired with an angelic bat of his lashes.

Like a moth to the flame, Abigail felt her gaze returning to Dylan's, felt herself being drawn into the fiery heat of his gaze.

"I do not use aspen trees for my work," Ziggy announced, reminding them both of his presence. "Pine is good, if prepared correctly." He lovingly ran his hand across the knots in the wood. "I have used linseed oil on this piece, you see how it glows?"

Dylan saw something glowing, all right. And it was in Abbie's sky blue eyes. He'd seen hunger; he'd seen desire. He'd seen enough to give him hope.

After dinner that night, Abigail was sitting in the upstairs bedroom she'd turned into an office, trying to edit what she'd written the day before, when the sound of someone softly playing a guitar came floating up through her open window. She managed to type a few more sentences on her computer screen before the sirenlike music sent her from her ergonomically designed office chair to the window to see who was playing.

Even pressing her nose against the glass, Abigail still couldn't see the covered porch that ran across the front and around the western corner of the ranch house. Reminding herself that she had to finish this chapter by that night, she dutifully returned to her chair, only to have the alluring music continue.

She lasted another fifteen minutes before tossing in the towel, using the excuse of a cold drink as a reason for going downstairs. After grabbing a bottle of kiwi-strawberry juice from the ancient fridge, she moseyed on outside.

She saw his boots first, propped up on the porch railing. She'd seen those same pointy-toed boots out of her peripheral vision right after she'd slipped from the rail and landed in the mud earlier that day. She was cleaned up now, and had changed into a floral skirt and pink top. The outfit made her feel feminine and was one she liked to write in; the fact that she looked rather nice in it was irrelevant, but did give her confidence as she raised her eyes to meet Dylan's mysterious dark gaze.

His only other audience was an orange barn cat, comfortably perched on the railing not far from his feet.

"Looks like you've got a friend," Abigail noted as she sat in the other pine rocker on the porch. Straightening the swing was still on her list of things to do. "That cat has kept its distance from me, but seems to have cottoned on to you."

"I've got a way with animals," Dylan admitted with something close to modesty.

"I'm not surprised. I was surprised to find you out here playing that, though," she said, pointing to the slightly battered guitar on his lap. She'd found it in the closet in the foreman's cabin and, since she wasn't a musician herself, had just left it there in case its owner ever returned.

"No more surprised than I am," he replied.

"What do you mean?"

"Let's just say I've never had a talent for music before. In fact, when I was a kid, the priest asked me not to sing while in church, but just to mouth the words. That's how bad I was."

"That's not a very nice thing to say to a child," Abigail said, indignant on his behalf.

"You've never heard me sing."

"Let me hear you now."

He just shook his head.

"Come on," she coaxed him. "I'll sing with you. Something easy. How about 'Home on the Range'?"

His version was somewhat unusual, including a line about antelopes not having much to say. But his voice was like liquid gold, rich and sexy. The man definitely could sing. Almost as well as he could kiss.

Try as she had, Abigail hadn't been able to forgot that kiss they'd shared in the mud earlier. It had been a for-get-your-name, melt-your-knees kind of kiss. And it had given her even more reasons to be tempted, and to be cautious. Her voice wavered and then petered out completely as she just sat there and listened to him. And stared at him.

By now, she knew exactly where the L-shaped rip was in his jeans and how much of his left thigh it exposed. Not enough. His hands strumming the guitar strings were calloused and nicked, his fingers lean and long and capable of creating pure magic—not only on a guitar but also on a woman's body. *Her* body.

Realizing she was eyeing him much too hungrily, she lowered her gaze to the cat while asking Dylan, ''Where did you learn to play?''

''Funny thing is that I just kinda picked it up over the past few days. I found this in the closet in the cabin, I hope you don't mind my playing it.''

''No, of course not. You must have a real ear for music, despite what your priest said.''

''Yeah, or maybe I'm just a late bloomer,'' Dylan said with a Gypsy grin.

''I doubt that,'' she replied. ''You seem pretty fast on the draw to me.''

''Not with you. Why, I've been here almost two weeks and haven't even asked you out yet,'' he said. ''There's a dance in Big Rock this Saturday night. How about stepping out with me?''

''Thanks, but I'd better not.''

''Why not? Don't tell me you're afraid?'' Dylan teased her. ''Of little ol' me?''

''Absolutely. Any wise woman would be, when her hormones . . .''

''Yeah? Go on,'' he prompted her, his grin now as wide as the sky.

Rather ticked off by the way he acted as if he knew exactly what she was thinking, she decided to say something guaranteed to scare him off. ''When a woman gets the nesting instinct. You know, wanting to settle down.'' That should send him running in the opposite direction, she told herself. ''A wise man would do well to watch his step then.''

''I'll do that, ma'am. I'm so glad we had this talk about the birds and the bees. Meanwhile, if you ever feel you need to stop fluttering around, and you're looking for a nest to settle in, you just fly on over to me and nest in my arms a spell.''

A spell. He was weaving one of those, all right. Snaring her with the white flash of his grin, the tempting curve of his darn-near perfect lips, the dark fire in his eyes. Gypsy eyes flashing Gypsy magic.

"Don't hold your breath," she muttered, tearing her eyes away.

"I noticed you do that when you kissed me. Hold your breath, I mean."

"I think it would be best if we both forgot that kiss happened."

"Not possible."

"Anything is possible. You just told me so yourself."

"If anything is possible, then it's possible you'll come with me for the dance in town this Saturday."

"I don't think that would be a good idea."

"Why not?"

"Because you're an employee of mine."

"Afraid I'm going to hit you with a sexual-harassment suit?"

"Of course not."

"Then what will it take for you to go out with me?"

"For you to be as rich as Croesus," she retorted in mocking exasperation.

Dylan just grinned at her.

But the next night, he came knocking on her front door—a stranger in tow. "This here is Buzz, Buzz Kreus. And he's got all of...how much was it again, Buzz?"

"Twenty-eight dollars and twenty-one cents."

"Twenty-eight dollars and twenty-one cents to his name."

"You expect me to believe that's his real surname?" she said in disbelief.

"Show her your driver's license, Buzz."

The older man flipped open a battered-looking wallet. Sure enough, his surname was Kresus—spelled differently than Croesus but pronounced the same way.

"Thank you, Buzz," Dylan said. "I reckon you can head on out now. And thanks again for stopping by. Good luck at that old-timers' rodeo up in Alberta."

"Sure thing, Dylan."

"Let's see..." Dylan counted out the money, his hand drawing her attention as he did so. He had long, slim, battle-scarred fingers. "That should be twenty-eight dollars and twenty-one cents. This is what you said it would take to make you go out with me to the dance this Saturday. Here you go."

She refused to take the money he held out. "I was talking about Croesus, spelled with a *C*...."

"Well, ma'am, then you should have been more specific. That's not what you said. No mention was made of spelling requirements. You just said—"

"I know what I said," she interrupted him.

"Good. Then I'll stop by to pick you up for the dance tomorrow around six."

Knowing when she was beaten, although assuring herself this was only a temporary setback even while she was wondering what to wear, Abigail said, "I won't be ready until six-thirty."

He allowed her her small victory. "Fine."

"Fine."

"It will be," he softly assured her. "Mighty fine." Reaching out, he briefly brushed one work-roughened fingertip down her cheek as he had done a number of times before. "Mighty fine indeed."

Abbie had written about physical attraction, had even experienced it personally before. But never to this degree, where one touch scattered her thoughts and her willpower like sparrows in the wind. Which made her a birdbrain for even considering taking up with a wandering cowboy like Dylan.

Despite Abigail's initial misgivings, she spent a great deal of time preparing for her date with Dylan. "It's not really a date," she told herself for about the hundredth time as she pawed through her closet.

"What else would you call it?" Raj asked from the doorway to Abigail's bedroom. The room was done in golden pine, which matched the rounded curve of the logs that formed the walls. Abigail had brought the eggshell-colored carpet with her. Not very practical for a ranch, she'd told Raj with a grin.

"You know, your carpet seems to be holding up better than you are," Raj noted.

Nodding, Abigail said, "I know."

"I think you should wear that short denim skirt with the flounce."

"And have every man in Big Rock looking at my thighs?" Abigail looked horrified at the very idea. "Forget it!"

"Are you worried about *every* man or about Dylan?" Raj inquired as she perched on the edge of a pine deacon's bench.

"What do you think?"

"That the two of you create some pretty powerful chemistry. And have you noticed how the hero in your latest book has taken on some of Dylan's characteristics?"

"Mule-headed stubbornness, you mean?"

"I was referring more to the perfect curve of his lips and the flash in his eyes. Or the way he slides his hand through his hair before stuffing his hat back on his head."

"Damn," Abigail groaned before sinking onto the bed. "I hadn't noticed that."

"Obviously you did notice Dylan doing that or you wouldn't have put it in the book."

"I meant I didn't realize I'd incorporated that into my book. What am I going to do?"

"Get dressed. Dylan will be here in another fifteen minutes."

"You're sure you don't want to come with us?"

"You've never heard that three is a crowd? Besides, I've got a hot date with Clint tonight."

"Clint who?"

"Clint Eastwood, of course, is there any other? There is a retrospective on cable tonight with episodes from 'Rawhide' and then the movies *For a Few Dollars More, Hang 'Em High* and *High Plains Drifter.*"

"I've got my own high-plains drifter to deal with tonight," Abigail muttered as she zipped up her denim skirt, the one with the more respectable hemline. She only had one pair of dress boots, so that made that choice easy. The fringe on her hot pink silk shirt rippled as she leaned over to tug her boots on. "And he's as clever as a coyote," she tacked on, remembering how Dylan had conned her into accepting his invitation tonight.

"Don't forget cuter than a moose," Raj inserted with a grin.

"Sure, *you* can laugh. You'll be curled up with a bowl of popcorn and Clint tonight."

"You know, I'm surprised your uncle had a satellite dish installed out here, considering how run-down the ranch house and all was."

"Shem told me he heard that Dylan got it for my uncle a few years back."

"That was generous of Dylan."

"I never said he couldn't be generous. That doesn't change the fact that he's a cowboy, and I am not getting involved with another cowboy."

"For all your complaining, you know you're going to have a great time tonight."

"You know, I've decided that it must be inbred in these cowboys to chase after anything that runs. I mean, think about it. They're used to chasing after cows and calves, rounding them up. Everything is a competition. To see who lasts the longest."

"Sounds like that could get *real* interesting," Raj stated with a wicked grin.

Abigail threw a pillow at her. "Stop that! I'm trying to be serious here. Maybe if I stopped running, Dylan would stop chasing. What do you think?"

"I think that's him at the door downstairs now. Here, you forgot to put on your left earring." Raj handed her the sterling-silver-and-turquoise-conch earring.

"What I really need to put on is a chastity belt," Abigail muttered.

"Might come in handy after the way you and Dylan were kissing up a storm in the corral the other day."

Abigail stopped short on her way downstairs, causing Raj to bump into her on the way down. "You saw that?"

"It was kind of hard to miss."

"Great. Who else saw? Have Shem or his sons said anything?"

"They were out fixing fences, remember? At least Shem's sons were."

"Thank heavens. What are you doing?" she demanded as Raj suddenly reached out to undo the top two buttons on Abigail's shirt.

"If you're going to stop running in the hopes of getting Dylan to stop chasing you, then you'd better loosen up a little."

"Right." Reaching around for the collar, Abigail turned it up and tossed her hair back, leaving a shadowy valley of cleavage just barely visible. The silver bear-claw necklace she wore was a personal good-luck charm. She had a feeling she'd need it tonight.

Another impatient knock on the front door reminded her that she still hadn't greeted Dylan yet. Belatedly opening the door, she felt her breath actually catch in her throat as she just stood there and stared at Dylan.

He looked good enough to eat. He'd dressed up, or as much as a cowboy dressed up, wearing crisp jeans and a starched white shirt with a black leather bola tie that had a sterling bear-claw clasp that matched the design of her necklace. How could he have known? She hadn't worn the necklace in front of him before. Of course, the design *was* a popular one. But still it was a little unnerving, almost as if it were a sign that this date—or whatever it was—was meant to be.

"You look good," Dylan murmured.

"So do you," she replied.

"Thank you, ma'am," he said, tipping back his hat with the tip of his right thumb. "Are you ready?"

Ready, willing and able. The wayward thought came to mind before Abigail could squelch it.

"Now, you kids be good," Raj teasingly called out after them.

"I'm always good," Dylan stated.

"And you're even better when you're bad, right?" Abigail drawled, giving Dylan his first inkling that there was something different about Abbie tonight. He'd noticed the undone buttons on her shirt right away, just as he'd noticed the way the silky fringe drew his attention to her breasts. Not that it took much to get his attention—everything about her seemed to strike a match inside of him, setting him off.

As he helped her into his pickup, Dylan recalled the last time she'd been in his truck, after he'd saved her that first day. There hadn't been any other unusual occurrences on the ranch since then, despite Hoss's warning that they'd better watch themselves. But then, Dylan had taken precautions, including installing a new floodlight for the ranch yard. After all, a man couldn't be too careful, at least not when he was responsible for a woman's safety. Especially when that woman was Abbie.

The dance was held at the community center, a fancy name for a concrete-block building that was the site for everything from bingo games to the Ranchers' Association meetings. A plaque near the front door proclaimed the fact that in 1947 Hoss Redkins's father had had the place built for the good of the community. It was just another indication of how powerful the Redkinses were in this county, and had been for decades. They were used to getting whatever they wanted. And in this case, Hoss Redkins wanted her ranch.

"Hondo and Randy told me they were coming to the festivities tonight," Dylan told her as he courteously held open the center's front door for her, keeping one arm around her shoulders while he used his free hand to deal with the tricky door handle. Apparently the Redkinses hadn't made any improvements on the structure since it had been built right after World War II. "If Hondo dances the way he eats, we're in trouble," he added.

A band was already in full swing, belting out old-fashioned country classics. Abigail hadn't stepped but four feet inside before Dylan had swept her into a northern version of the Texas two-step.

The place was crowded, forcing Abigail and Dylan even closer together. Not that Dylan needed any forcing. He was happy having her in his arms. "You're good," he said in her ear, needing to lean that close to be heard over the music, which was now a George Strait hit.

"So are you," Abigail replied, having to turn her head to do so. Which is how her lips ended up mere millimeters from his. Her steps faltered, and she nearly stepped on his toes.

"Hang on, there." Dylan's voice was rich and it trickled down her spine like warm brandy. "Things should slow down in a minute or two."

Things... like her heart? It was racing.

Sure enough, the band finished up that number and then went into a slow ballad about a man who done a woman wrong.

Instead of just placing his arm around her shoulder or her waist, as he had for the Western shuffle they'd just finished, Dylan took her firmly into his arms, arms that had no business feeling so much like home. They danced cheek to cheek. The gentle abrasion of his skin against hers was a wondrous thing. She suspected he'd shaved before picking her up, but there was still an intrinsic difference between the texture of his lean jaw and hers. Her fingers clung to his shoulder, appreciating the lanky warmth beneath the crisp cotton shirt. Temptation loomed large. She was tempted to close her eyes, tempted to run her lips along the line of his jaw, tempted to throw his hat over her shoulder and run her fingers through his midnight black hair.

It took three taps on Dylan's shoulder for him to notice that Randy was standing there with an expectant look on his face. "Beat it," Dylan growled.

"That wasn't very friendly," Abigail noted as with a grumble and a frown Randy retreated.

"Damn right. He can find his own girl."

By the time the dance was over, Abigail's mouth was dry and her heart was doing a two-step of its own. As if taking pity on her overexcited state, the band took a fifteen-minute break. Waving a hand in front of her face, she breathlessly stated, "It's warm in here."

"How about a cold drink?"

"That sounds great, thanks."

"You stay here, and I'll go face the crowd," Dylan said with a nod at the people gathered around the metal washtub full of ice and cans of beer and soda.

As she stood waiting for him, Abigail tuned in to the conversations going on around her, one of the traits of being a writer. As if scanning the channels, Abigail heard and discarded various snatches of dialogue until one sentence caught her attention.

"I heard he has Gypsy blood," a bleached blonde standing nearby said.

When the woman went on to speculate what Dylan would be like as a lover, it was all Abigail could do not to smack her. But then, what else could she expect from a woman who wore no bra under her Girls Go Nuts For Cowboy Butts T-shirt?

To make matters worse, the hussy strutted on over to Dylan. As Abigail watched, the bleached blonde tugged on his arm. Having gotten Dylan's attention, the woman batted her lashes at him, not to mention jiggling her unbound breasts.

Abigail was itching to go over and growl, *Hands off, blondie, he's mine!*

In fact, she'd taken two steps forward before common sense intervened.

So what should she do instead? Mosey on over and juggle the woman's elbow so that she spilled soda all over her cowboy-butts shirtfront? But that wouldn't be very nice, and Abigail had been raised to be a good girl.

So what were her options here? To stand there and do nothing? No way!

What would one of her heroines do? Well, Loretta was hotheaded and she'd most likely...

"Sugar, the young 'uns are a'callin for their daddy out in the pickup," Abigail told Dylan in a drawl as thick as molasses. "Andy and Billy and Cal and Dudley and Eliot and Fred..."

"You've got six kids?" the blonde asked in surprise.

"Un-by-god-believable, huh?" Abigail said. "You must not be from around these parts, huh?"

"I'm from Great Falls."

"Sugar plum, she's from your old stomping grounds," Dylan said with a grin. "I wish we could talk longer, but you heard my woman here, the children are a'crying." Taking Abigail's arm, he led her away, having snagged two cans of soda before he did so.

Once they were alone in a far corner of the room, Dylan said, "Let me guess, that was right out of your book *Flame of the West,* right?"

"How do you know that?"

"I read it. Liked it pretty well, too."

There might be hope for this man after all, Abigail thought to herself with a smile.

"But couldn't you have come up with a better name than Fred?" Dylan demanded.

"What?"

"When you listed all our children, all of them boys, I might add. Don't you want any daughters?"

"I was just kidding."

"About naming our son Fred? That's reassuring."

"I'd name him Ferdinand instead," she said with a saucy toss of her head.

"You're good," he said with admiration.

"Come on, folks," the mustached lead singer of the band shouted into the microphone. "This here's the local-talent portion of our program. Any budding singers out there tonight, here's your chance to come on up here and join the band for a number."

Afterward Dylan was never quite sure how he ended up on stage, but he had the feeling that Abigail had given him a healthy shove in that direction. And so it was that he found himself singing "Shameless."

The lyrics took on a special meaning for Abigail as she listened to them sung in Dylan's rich and rough voice. The fact that he looked right at her the entire time merely doubled the effect, which left her knees weak.

By the time the song was over, he'd gained the attention of every woman in the place. The applause was raucous enough, but the cheers were downright rowdy.

"Thank y'all very much," Dylan said with a grin that made all the women in the crowd edge a little closer to the makeshift stage. "If my family could only see me now."

Abigail was *seeing* him now and she was having a hard time remembering her vow to avoid cowboys at all costs. Surely there were some things worth the risk—and right at that moment, Dylan looked good enough to be one of them.

When he hopped down from the stage and hooked her in his arms, she returned his embrace.

"Let's get out of here," he whispered in her ear.

Moments later, they were outside, kissing under the Milky Way, his tempting tongue sending shooting stars through her body as he tickled the corners of her lips.

Accepting his invitation to passion, she slid her hands up his chest to his shoulders. The pressure of his mouth on hers was gentle until she tilted his hat out of her way. She wanted to toss his black Stetson over her shoulder and run her fingers through his too-long hair, but knew that cowboys were funny about their hats. Not that Dylan let it get in his way. No, he was actually quite creative about the angle of his kiss.

The rough moistness of his tongue diverted her thoughts and consumed her senses. Sighing his name, she parted her lips. He had one hand on her waist, his fingers spread widely apart so that his thumb almost brushed her left breast. His other hand cupped her head, his fingers threaded through her hair while his thumb tenderly grazed her cheek.

One kiss blended into the next, each increasing in intensity, growing with slow hunger and steady anticipation. They were completely wrapped up in each other, and in each other's arms, when the sound of raucous laughter shattered the moment.

"Well, looky here, if it ain't the gimpy Gypsy. Looks like he's tryin' to romance his way into getting a piece of old man Turner's ranch," Hoss Redkins derided.

Five

Abigail felt Dylan tense in her arms before he whirled to face Hoss Redkins and his equally burly son, Hoss Jr.

Remembering the last time that Dylan and Hoss had faced off, Abigail hung on to Dylan's arm for all she was worth. "Ignore him," she whispered to Dylan. "He's just an old windbag looking for trouble."

"And he's found it," Dylan growled.

"Don't give him the satisfaction."

"What about my satisfaction?"

"You're better than he is. You have the willpower to walk away."

"You need permission from your boss lady before you talk?" Hoss taunted Dylan, who took another step toward him with menace in his eyes. "And don't you go thinking you can practice any more of that black magic—I'm not riding a horse and I've got protection this time." Hoss nodded at his son and two ranch hands who'd materialized nearby. "We don't want your kind around here."

Furious, Abigail yelled at Hoss, "There's no protection for what ails you—a bigoted, small-minded idiot who gives ranchers everywhere a bad name!"

"Now who's trying to start a fight?" Dylan murmured with dry humor.

"That's why women don't make good ranchers," Hoss stated. "Because they're so emotional. They take things personally. Why don't you do us both a favor and stop this nonsense now, before things get sticky? I've made you a generous offer for your uncle's run-down ranch. You'd be well-advised to accept it. Your daddy thinks it's the right thing to do—"

"You talked to my father?" Abigail said in disbelief.

"Of course I did," Hoss confirmed. "I thought maybe he could talk some sense into you."

"My father doesn't own the Tumbling T Ranch. I do. And there's no way I'd sell it to you!"

"Now don't go making hysterical statements you might later regret," Hoss said. "You don't want to make an enemy out of me. And I think that you'll soon find out that you've bitten off more than you can chew here. Your daddy did the smart thing selling his half of the ranch off to me all those years ago. You'll do the same in the end."

"Don't hold your breath."

"I won't have to. All I have to do is hold the water. The irrigation lines from the river go through my land, you know."

She hadn't.

"One word from me and you won't be able to boil a cup of water, take any of those fancy baths or water your cattle. Unless you plan on coming into town and buying bottles of that fancy bottled water for them," Hoss added before laughing heartily at his own humor. "I hear them cows like fancy foreign water—the one with all the bubbles." His guffaw could be heard clear over the border to Canada. "So you think long and hard before you say no to my offer again. And you be mighty careful out on that ranch, I wouldn't want anything happening to you or them strange foreign friends of yours."

"Nothing is going to happen to them," Dylan said, his voice as hard as his expression. "Because if it does, I'll come looking for you before you can even haul your carcass down off your horse."

"Ooooh, boys, did you hear that? Lord, I'm just about shivering in my boots," Hoss mocked.

"Or I could just call down a Gypsy curse on you right now," Dylan reflected. "Preventative medicine, so to speak."

Hoss looked disconcerted before blustering on, "I'm wearing garlic. You can't touch me!"

"I don't need to touch you. And garlic only works on vampires."

"I've heard it's also useful in preventing you from getting a cold," Abigail inserted, trying to keep a straight face.

"I don't get colds," Hoss bragged.

"I'm glad to hear that. Enjoy your good health while you can," Dylan drawled. "A man in your condition can't be too careful." Lowering his eyebrows, Dylan fixed Hoss with a deadly glare. "You ever heard of the evil eye, Redkins?"

Hoss clutched his garlic and took a step backward, bumping into his burly son.

"Dad, you stepped on my foot!" Hoss Jr. yowled, hopping on one foot and grabbing his other in his hands. "I think you broke it!"

"It's his fault! He gave me the evil eye," Hoss exclaimed, pointing a shaking finger at Dylan. "You're witnesses, boys. I'm going to the sheriff with this," he warned before helping his son into the community center. "Don't just stand there!" he yelled at his ranch hands. "Get a move on and help my son inside." At the doorway, he turned to shout one final warning, "You've gone too far this time, Janos! You're going to pay for this!"

"Come on, let's go," Dylan said, taking her arm and leading her to his pickup.

"Can he really turn off the water?" Abigail quietly asked.

"I don't know. I'll check it out. But I have a feeling that if it was that easy, he'd have done that to Pete years ago."

Dylan had a point, she noted.

"It's more likely that he's bluffing, trying to panic you into selling."

"It won't work. I don't panic easily."

"Unless you're in my arms," Dylan noted as they reached his truck. "I wonder why that is?"

"I didn't panic tonight."

"No. Makes me wonder why."

"Maybe I decided to stop running."

"And maybe you've come up with some other plan."

"And what plan might that be?"

"Who knows? A woman like you, one with plenty of imagination, is bound to come up with something."

"It sounds to me as if you're the one with the overactive imagination," she stated.

"So you're saying you're ready to go to bed with me?" he countered.

"No!"

"How about making love beneath the stars?"

"Love wouldn't enter into it. You're talking about sex."

"It's a part of life."

"You specialize in leaving. Not in living," she told him. Or loving, she thought to herself.

"We all leave—one way or another, one time or another. That's why we have to enjoy the moments we have."

"So men have been telling women since prehistoric times. They go off, following their code of honor, fighting wars, conquering lands and other women. And who is left behind to clean up the mess? The woman. Besides, you're younger than I am."

Her non sequitur threw him. "What?"

"You heard me."

"So I'm younger. What's that got to do with anything?"

"I'm not looking for a one-night stand. At this point in my life, I'm looking for a little security...."

"Which is why you quit your comfortable job down in Great Falls and moved up here to take over your uncle's ranch."

"Okay, I'm allowed a few contradictions in my life, but you're not going to be one of them."

"And why's that?"

"Because I said so. Look, I know this is some kind of game for you, a challenge like staying in the saddle eight seconds."

"Oh, I can last longer than eight seconds," he assured her with a naughty grin.

"I've heard it all before, cowboy."

"Not from me, you haven't."

"And what makes you different?" she countered.

"This." Swooping down, he captured her lips in a sizzling kiss. Where before he'd teased her, slowly building the fire, this time he consumed her, igniting a passion that was comet hot.

The summer wind swirled around them, and his tongue swirled around hers, fanning more flames. His embrace was tight, pressing her against his aroused body, letting her feel just how much he wanted her.

Lifting his lips from hers, he murmured, "This is something special, it's not like anything else, not like being with anyone else. This is just you and me."

"And chemistry," she said, taking a shaky step away.

"Or magic," he whispered.

Abigail shook her head, her long curly hair falling into her eyes. "I don't believe in magic."

Dylan smoothed a tendril away from her eyelashes as he noted, "You write about love and you don't believe in magic?"

"Not the kind you're practicing."

"And what kind might that be?"

"The temporary kind." And with those words, she got into the truck's cab and slammed the door.

The forty-minute ride back to the ranch was done in silence, broken by the Chris LeDoux tape that Dylan turned on after the first fifteen minutes. Almost every song was centered on rodeo life, reinforcing Abigail's initial misgivings and Dylan's sense of what he'd lost.

"This is ridiculous," Dylan said as he turned off the ignition and the cassette at the same time.

"I'm glad you finally realize that," she replied.

"Why do I have the feeling we're not talking about the same thing?"

"Because it seems we're *never* talking about the same thing. You're only interested in one thing. And we both know what that is."

"It used to be saddle-bronc riding," Dylan noted harshly as he took off his hat to shove his hand through his hair before setting his broad-rimmed black Stetson in place again.

Seeing the mannerism made her own weakness strike home. As far as he was concerned, rodeo still came first. "Are you missing the buckle bunnies hanging on your every word?"

"My words weren't what they hung on to, honey."

Abigail felt a flash of something suspiciously like jealousy streak through her. "I'm sure. And I'm sure you enjoyed every second of it."

"I like a little fun as much as the next man, but these days you'd have to be crazy to go risking your life acting on every invitation."

"This from a man who risked his life every time he got into the rodeo ring."

"It's not as dangerous as all that."

"Right," she scoffed.

"It's not. No more so than football."

"Oh, that's real reassuring," she mocked.

"Are you worried about me?"

"Should I be?"

"It looks like my rodeo days are behind me now," he noted with that trace of bitterness she picked up on right away.

"But you'd give anything to be back, for another go-round, for another chance to break your neck."

Dylan shrugged. "It goes with the territory. Haven't you ever wanted anything enough to risk everything to go after it?"

"I've taken my share of risks."

"There you go, then."

"But I only took those risks when I knew I had a good chance of succeeding."

"I did have a good chance of succeeding. Hell, I had a damn good chance of winning at nationals again this year! I was second in the national standings before I busted up my leg." He rubbed his thigh with a clenched hand.

"Did the dancing tonight aggravate it?"

"No, the dancing damn well didn't aggravate it," he growled. "If you want to know what's aggravating me, it's you."

"Me? What did I do?"

"Kiss me like you meant it and then act like nothing happened." A grin suddenly flashed across his dark countenance as he drawled, "Lucky for you, I'm a forgiving kind of guy."

"Oh, yeah, you're just the model of patience," she mockingly retorted.

"Which is why I can do this—" he brushed a quick kiss across her cheek "—and walk away afterward. Good night." Tipping his hat, he was on his way, merrily whistling under his breath.

"Listen, cowboy, I already know you're a pro at walking away!" Abigail shouted after him. He was also a pro at kissing, but she had no intention of imparting that information.

She'd stomped up the porch to sit on the still-crooked swing before realizing that—to her surprise—Dylan had come back to her. On a roll now, she continued her diatribe. "Men have forgotten how to be romantic, if they ever knew how in the first place!"

"That's not true. Men can be just as romantic as women."

"I have yet to meet one."

"You're looking at one right now."

"You?"

"Yes, me. You don't believe me?"

"Say something romantic. Go ahead and give it your best shot."

"All right." Taking her hand in his and looking her straight in the eyes, he softly murmured, "I want you to know that there are probably a hundred thousand things about you that I admire, but the thing that really makes me proud to be the man sitting here beside you is the fact that you believe in me and I believe in you."

Abigail's heart stopped. She forgot to breathe. He made her believe, believe in magic, in anything being possible, including the fact that he was speaking the truth.

That was before the glint of humor in his Gypsy eyes brought her back to earth.

Snatching her hand away, she said, "You're a smooth talker. That's different from being romantic."

"So I'm supposed to stutter and search around for words instead of saying what I feel?"

"You weren't telling me how you feel."

"How do you know?"

"Because you were just kidding around."

"This just confirms the point I was making. Women make it almost impossible for a man to show he's romantic. Because they don't believe he's telling them the truth."

"So, you were just trying to make a point. I knew it."

"You're impossible!" he growled.

"Hey, do you mind if I use that romantic line in a book?" she couldn't resist calling after him.

"The one about you being impossible? Go right ahead!" Dylan had ended up having the last word, after all.

The next day was Sunday, Dylan's day off. It didn't start out well.

For one thing, he knocked over the Gypsy box, but thankfully it fell on a pile of his dirty clothes so it wasn't damaged. His sister would skin him alive if he ruined the family treasure. And that got him to thinking, realizing that in his intentness on Abbie he hadn't called home in several weeks. The phone in the cabin was from the fifties, but it did work.

"What state are you in this time?" his mother asked him after first making sure that he was okay and eating well. If she fussed this much over him while thinking he was healthy, he could just imagine what a hyper state she'd be in if she knew about his injury.

"What state are you in?" his mother repeated.

A state of confusion, Dylan thought to himself, combing his hair back out of his still-sleepy eyes as he remembered the emotional roller-coaster ride he'd been on with Abbie last night. "I'm in northern Montana." He gave her the address and the ranch phone number. "I'll be here the rest of the summer."

"The rest of the summer? That's not like you, Dylan. Are you doing all right?"

"I'm doing fine."

"Your brother is here with Brett and the baby. Wait, he wants to talk to you."

"Hey, Dylan, good to hear from you," Michael said. "Fallen off any horses lately?" he mocked as he did each time he talked to Dylan.

Ignoring the stab of pain at the memory of his last fall, Dylan answered him with equal fraternal mockery. "No, but I rode to the rescue of a damsel in distress."

"Sounds interesting."

"She is. She's trying to hold on to her ranch, and someone else wants her off of it. So they put a few burrs under her horse's saddle."

"Have you notified the authorities?"

"With what? Suspicions? No. Besides, the main suspect owns the neighboring ranch, along with a good portion of the county."

Michael's voice was dead serious as he said, "Do you think this suspect will try something worse next time?"

"Could be."

"Damn it, Dylan, that doesn't sound like a very stable situation."

"Hey, you know me. I thrive on danger and excitement."

"And I've dealt with people who will do anything to get what they want. I track them down in my security business, remember? Give me the guy's name, and I'll run a security check on him."

"His name is Hoss Redkins."

"What a name. I'm getting this image . . ."

"Of an overindulged, overblown buffoon? That's him. And I can tell you that his belly is a real giveaway. No true rancher carries around a tire like that. They work too damn hard."

"Well, don't *you* work too damn hard," Michael said. "And call our sister. Right away. She's been on my back about not hearing from you. She's just about ready to have me get out a search party to look for you. So check in more often and give her a call right now, before she drives me nuts."

Dylan lasted all of about three minutes talking to Gaylynn before letting something slip. They were discussing the Rom box. "If it granted wishes, I'd wish for my career back," Dylan joked.

"Back?" Gaylynn repeated in confusion. "What do you mean back?"

"Nothing. Never mind. It was a joke."

"No way I'm buying that, little brother. You might as well tell me now, because you know I'll just hound it out of you in the end. And I should warn you that I've learned a few things from the master of hounding inquisition, Hunter Davis himself."

"And how are you and your new husband doing?"

"Just fine, and don't try changing the subject. What happened with your bronc riding?"

"First you have to swear that you won't tell Mama anything."

"You think I can't keep a secret? Hey, I'm not the one who spilled the beans about their surprise twentieth-wedding-anniversary party. That was you, remember?"

Dylan groaned. "You'll never let me forget. Okay, the thing is, I had a little accident...."

"What happened? Are you okay? Did you break anything? Are you in the hospital? Are you okay?"

"No, I'm not okay," Dylan said in exasperation. "I keep getting interrupted by my sister. If you'd be quiet a second, I'll tell you what happened."

"Then talk faster," she shot back.

"I bit the dust down in Arizona. Landed the wrong way and ended up busting my leg in a couple places. I'd already messed up my knee from an injury before...."

Anyway, the bottom line is that they told me I wouldn't be able to ride competitively again. Normally I'd ignore the doctors, but this time it looks like they're right."

"Oh, Dylan..."

"The doctors had told me I was lucky to have retained as much use of the leg as I have, lucky that I'm still able to ride at all. But I'll never ride like I did before." He fingered the championship gold belt buckle in its presentation box that he kept on the bedside table. "So forgive me if I don't feel real lucky, despite that magic box you sent."

"Oh, Dylan, I wish there was something I could say—"

He stopped her. "There isn't, but thanks anyway."

To his relief, she changed the subject. "You got the box safely, then?"

"You bet. Sorry I haven't been in touch before, to congratulate you on your marriage and all, but I haven't been real good company."

"Where are you?"

"Staying on a friend's ranch in northern Montana." He gave her the phone number. "Actually I'm working for a Western-romance writer. Abigail Turner. You ever heard of her?"

"Heard of her? I've read all her books! She's great! Wait a minute, what do you mean you're working for her? Doing what?"

"She's inherited this ranch from her uncle, a friend of mine who's passed on. She'd decided to try and run the place herself."

"With some help from you?"

"That's right."

"I thought your motto was not to get involved. Weren't you the one who told me that a cowboy's best life insurance was minding your own business?"

"That was before I met Abbie."

"Aha," Gaylynn murmured triumphantly.

"What was that 'aha' for?"

Instead of answering, she asked, "Did you open the magic box?"

"Yeah."

"And did you see anyone right after you opened it?"

"I was alone in my cabin."

"You didn't see anyone?"

"Abbie slipped off the fence in the corral...."

"So you saw Abbie," Gaylynn interrupted him. "And now you're talking about staying in one place...."

"Hey, who said anything about staying?"

"You are, aren't you?"

"For the summer, maybe, but I never..."

"Even the summer is a big step for a rolling stone like you. I can't remember the last time you stayed in one place for that long."

"Chasing rodeo means moving around a lot."

"And now you're chasing Abbie instead."

"What makes you think she hasn't fallen head over heels in love with me already?" Dylan retorted. "Isn't that what this magic box of yours is supposed to do?"

"The box belongs to the family, not just me. Have you talked to Michael about how it affected him?"

"No way."

"Men," Gaylynn snorted in disgust. "Well, much as he might say that Brett is the one who swears by the box's magic, let me tell you he's not such a doubter himself. Not after every baby in a mile's radius seems to be drawn to him as if he were a baby magnet or something. You read my letter, about the secondary effect, right? About your gaining a skill you never had before?''

"Yeah, and you'll get a kick out of this. I was on stage last night at a dance and I was singing.''

Gaylynn groaned. "How fast did you empty the place out?''

"That's the thing. All of a sudden, my voice sounds pretty darn good.''

"See, that's what I mean! It's the box working.''

"Well, I hate to burst your bubble, sis, but the truth is that I was attracted to Abbie even before I got the box.''

"And what about her? How does she feel about you?''

"She hasn't quite reconciled herself to the inevitable conclusion yet...."

"Meaning she's putting up one hell of a fight," Gaylynn translated wryly.

"She's got this thing against cowboys. Says we only know about leaving, not about living.''

"She does have a way with words, doesn't she?" Gaylynn said with admiration. "Sounds like you've got your work cut out for you.''

"I'll win her over in the end.''

"And then what? What happens when the summer is over?''

"How should I know?''

"Fight it all you want, Dylan, but I think your rolling-stone days are numbered.''

"Wait a minute. Hold on to your horses, there. The Gypsy legend talks about falling in love. Nothing about getting married and settling down.''

"What's to stop you from marrying her if you're both in love?''

He shifted uncomfortably. "You're getting ahead of things here. I only met her two weeks ago.''

"Brett and Michael only knew each other less than a month before getting married."

"That was for the baby," Dylan argued. "To keep Hope."

"And don't *you* give up hope, little brother," Gaylynn told him. "I know how much rodeo meant to you, but God works in mysterious ways. When He closes a door, somewhere He opens a window. Maybe Abigail Turner is your window. Your ultimate destiny."

My destiny, Dylan thought to himself. Or my downfall?

Six

Abigail tilted her head to reread what she'd just typed on her computer screen. The writing *wasn't* going well.

Trying not to get discouraged, she popped another handful of cherry jelly beans into her mouth and curled her toes into the plush rug beneath her feet. She'd never been able to write while wearing shoes or even socks. It had to be bare feet.

When she'd done a writer's workshop at the Romance Writers of America's conference last year, she'd talked about the mysterious magic of writing and the steps writers sometimes took, which made superstitious ball players seem tame in comparisons. Abigail knew writers who had crystals on their desks, positive affirmations tacked onto their walls, photographs of inspiring places or people stuck to every spare inch of wall space.

And when things weren't going well, like today, then sometimes desperate measures were called for, including changing the color on the video monitor, moving to another room, changing chairs or reverting to the tools of the old days—pen and paper.

When things got rocky, Abigail always tried to reassure herself by mentally saying she was in the construction business, *word* construction. She did that because there were times when being a *writer* was just too darn scary. What if the magic never came back? What if she couldn't write another book? What if she ran out of things to say?

Then we'll do the talking, her heroine reassured her.

Abigail grinned. She'd often said that her characters were very real to her, and she was just sitting there taking notes as they had their wild adventures. She just wished they'd learn how to type!

In the end, she got a good three hours' worth of work done before realizing that she was at it again, bestowing Dylan's characteristics onto her hero, Jake—who'd started the book with light brown hair and blue eyes and now had flashing dark eyes and long dark hair. He was even starting to sound like Dylan. "Don't tell me you're afraid of little ol' me," she'd just typed.

Just for fun, she had her heroine steal the clothes that her hero had left on the riverbank and burn them.

Abigail's grin was short-lived as she got to wondering what Dylan would look like, standing stark naked in a stream that only went to just below his navel. Droplets of water would run from his dampened, long dark hair, lazily meandering over his shoulders, down his chest and washboard stomach. His grin would be temptation enough to kiss it from his mouth. She'd run her fingers through his hair, down his back, beneath the water to...

Abigail's fingers flew as she wrote a heated love scene, not even noticing that she'd typed Dylan's name instead

of her hero's until she'd finished it and completion had
been reached, by her heroine if not herself.

No, Abigail was still seething with unfulfilled desire.
Her eyes wandered on over to the window and the horse
corral she could see outside. Dylan was there, in the open
doorway to the barn, using a pitchfork, appropriately
enough for a man who had such a devilish grin.

He looked good enough to eat. He'd taken off his
shirt. She could barely make out the ripple of his back
muscles as he leaned into the pitchfork for another load
of hay. Her mouth watered at the way his jeans rode low
on his hips. Where were her binoculars when she needed
them?

She was as bad as that woman who'd worn the Girls
Go Nuts For Cowboy Butts T-shirt. But that didn't stop
her from looking.

Dylan's body seemed to be a magnet that pulled at her,
creating an irresistible force field tugging her ever closer.
She was mesmerized by the fluidity of his movements,
which were nothing fancy but were totally self-assured,
projecting confidence and skill and...sex. Abigail
couldn't get her mind off it. Or him.

The thought that this might be more than just physical attraction scared her even more. Chemistry was a
powerful thing. When combined with love, it was downright overpowering.

Not that Abigail would be foolish enough to fall for a
rolling stone like Dylan. If his injury hadn't taken him
out of the rodeo circuit, he'd be off at some rodeo right
now, never giving her a second thought. He'd made her
no promises, probably because he hadn't wanted to lie—
to say he'd always be there for her when she'd be lucky if
he hadn't left by the end of August.

One summer. That's all she'd have with him. Barely two months. It wouldn't be enough. She knew that. Just as she knew that kissing him hadn't been enough. She'd wanted more, and so had he. But that's where the similarity had ended. Dylan wanted sex, uncomplicated by emotions and declarations of unending love. She wanted more.

Despite his injury, Dylan wasn't done wandering. He certainly wasn't ready to settle down yet. She knew that, but turning away from the passion he promised her was almost impossible, and getting tougher by the minute.

Drooling over him this way wasn't helping things, she reminded herself even as she stole one last look. The thing to do was to keep things cool and businesslike between them. Rancher to ranch foreman.

Abigail tried to do that during dinner that night, but got distracted by the feel of his fingers brushing hers as he passed the gravy, not to mention passing the candied carrots and the salad. He kept handing her bowls whether she wanted them or not. And each time, he took the opportunity to add a softly diverting touch.

When he played the guitar outside her window after dinner, she tried putting on headphones and playing her portable CD player loudly. That didn't help much.

Unable to stand the suspense when the music outside stopped, she rolled her chair over to the window to see what was going on. She saw Dylan leaning against the railing around the corral. His horse, Traveler, was nuzzling his shoulder, something Abigail wouldn't mind doing herself.

As she watched, Dylan nimbly stepped up on the rail to wind his fingers in Traveler's dark mane. A second later, he was astride, riding bareback around the corral before leaning over to undo the gate leading to the open meadows.

As she watched the sky turn scarlet, Dylan rode off into the sunset in true Hollywood Western fashion. The scenery provided a spectacular backdrop, one that would have done director John Ford proud. The cloud formations were those her father had called mare's tails, brilliant streaks of sunlit crimson. The play of light over the mountains defined them, making the range of the northern Rockies seem much closer than they actually were.

Such grand scenery might make a man seem inconsequential. Not so Dylan. He was an integral part of it all; the silhouette of man and horse riding wild across the open valley was the very embodiment of the West.

When Abigail almost rolled over her bare toe with her chair in an effort to get a last look at Dylan, she knew she had to put a stop to this. She had to get her mind off Dylan and back on track. She had a book to write and a ranch to protect. People were counting on her. Raj, Ziggy, Shem, her editor, her agent. Time to get back to work.

But when Raj came in later that night, with chapter six in her hands, Abigail knew her tactics weren't working.

"You forgot to take Dylan's name off of the love scene on page ninety-nine," Raj said, managing a straight face for all of two seconds before cracking up.

"It's a good thing you're a close friend of mine, or I'd be tempted to murder you," Abigail muttered darkly.

"I've heard sexual frustration can do that to a person."

"This isn't funny! Nothing I've tried has worked," Abigail wailed. "I tried treating him like an employee...."

"That you lust after..."

"I've tried treating him like a friend...."

"That you lust after..." Raj repeated.

"I've even given him the green light so he wouldn't keep chasing me. At the dance, I kissed him back when he kissed me, and just got into more trouble. I tried scaring him off with talk of settling down and a woman's nesting instincts."

"And?"

"And he just told me to nest in his arms for a spell. I swear the man has cast a spell on me. I'm not normally like this." Getting up, Abigail began prowling around her office. "Sure, I've had a weakness for cowboys before, but it's never been anything like this. This is all-consuming. This is never-ending. This is..."

"The real thing?" Raj quietly asked.

"What if it is?" Abigail whispered back.

"Would that be so bad?"

"Not while Dylan was here, no. But when he takes off, yes, it would be. Like having my heart torn out and stomped on by a herd of wild horses."

"It's going to take a herd of wild horses to keep you two apart. Some things were meant to be. Fate, you know. Destiny."

"Fate means for me to be miserable? Why? What did I ever do to it?"

"So what are you going to do?"

"I considered trying to act like he was my younger brother."

Raj snorted derisively.

"Yeah, that's what I thought," Abigail morosely agreed. "That would last all of about five minutes. If only I knew what to do, if only I got a sign somehow..."

As if on cue, the lights suddenly went out. Since it was after ten, the room went pitch-dark. "Great!" Abigail muttered as she reached for the flashlight she kept on her bookcase. "I didn't back up that last page. Not that I'd written anything brilliant on it." She turned off her computer equipment so that there wouldn't be a power surge through it when the electricity came back on. "That wasn't the kind of sign I was looking for," she announced to the heavens.

"What do you think happened to the electricity?" Raj asked.

"I don't know. Out here, anything could have happened to it."

"They were going to have *The Boot Hill Brigade,* you know, that 1937 Western classic—"

"That no one has seen but you," Abigail interjected.

"—on cable at midnight."

"Don't you ever sleep?" Abigail asked Raj in amazement, knowing darn well that her friend got up at five-thirty in the morning to prepare breakfast for the men. Before they'd moved up here, Raj had insisted on taking over the cooking duties, since Abigail was providing all the food.

"You should talk," Raj retorted. "I've heard you up here pacing in your room until all hours of the morning."

"I'm worrying about the book," Abigail said. "And the ranch and everything."

"Dylan being a major part of that *everything,* right?"

"Wrong. Dylan is all of that *everything,*" Abigail wryly admitted. "But don't count me down-and-out just yet. This, too, shall pass."

* * *

But by the next morning, Abigail suffered another setback. It started out with her watching Dylan with Traveler out her office window. The two moved as one. Then something went wrong. Traveler suddenly reared and bucked as if competing in a saddle-bronc competition. All four of the horses' hooves left the ground as the gelding arched his back in a perfect inverted U.

To Abigail's amazement, Dylan managed to stay in the saddle. She would have gone running outside to make sure he was okay, but her knees suddenly turned into mush and she dropped onto her office chair with a thump.

He's all right, she kept repeating like a chant. *Dylan is fine.*

"You're not doing so good, though," she told herself in disgust. "Look at you." She held up her trembling hands. "What a sissy reaction! Get a hold of yourself!"

Problem was, she'd rather get a hold of Dylan!

"Abbie, Dylan wants to talk to you," Raj called from downstairs a few minutes later.

"Is he okay?"

"He's fine. A wasp stung his horse."

Remembering an old cowboy cure she'd read about, she yelled down. "Give him some of my uncle's chewing tobacco to use on the sting and tell him I'll meet him out in the barn in a few minutes."

By then, Abigail hoped to have her act together. She did, but it crumbled when the first thing Dylan said was, "I know what you're thinking."

Abigail sure hoped not! If so, he'd know she still hadn't recovered yet—from the eye-fest she'd had yesterday afternoon and the fall he'd almost taken this morning. Today he wore a shirt, light blue and white checked, with his jeans. It didn't matter. She already knew what his chest looked like, and she was free to imagine....

"You're thinking that I forgot about checking into Redkins's threat about cutting the water for the irrigation lines," Dylan said.

Abigail nodded, because after all, that would have been her second choice.

"The only irrigation lines that are fed from the river on his land are those in the northeastern corner of the ranch. And that meadow is fallow now, Pete hasn't planted anything there for over two years now. The water here on the ranch comes from a well. I took the liberty of beefing up the lighting near our well, just in case Redkins takes it into his mind to tamper with our main water supply."

Chilled at the possibility, Abigail ran her hands over her arms.

"Hondo, Randy and I are taking turns doing a night watch," Dylan continued. "Shem wasn't too pleased at not being included, claimed I was discriminating against him because of his age."

"What did you say?"

"That I was rewarding him because of his seniority and years of experience."

"And he said?"

"Not to do him any favors," Dylan allowed wryly. "So I gave in and let him take one of the night watches."

"He was just following the Western code of behavior," Abigail said. "Otherwise known as mule-headed stubbornness. You might have recognized the symptoms," she tacked on mockingly.

"Having observed them in you, you mean?" he retorted with a grin.

"I guess I should have seen that one coming," she wryly acknowledged.

"All kidding aside, we've got to keep our guard up around here. Redkins already cut off the water to that pasture. Like I said, it's just lucky that we're not using the land now."

"Which he must know."

Dylan nodded. "That power cut last night was deliberate. The power crew was out at dawn and they told me it looked like one of the main lines to the house was cut."

"Shouldn't we tell the sheriff in Big Rock about that?"

"I tried to. Called him up this morning, but he just said there wasn't enough proof. And then he muttered something about harmless vandalism, that teenagers must have gotten bored and decided to raise a little hell."

"Redkins has been very clever, I'll give him that. He hasn't done anything that can be traced back to him. I heard a wasp stung Traveler."

Dylan nodded. "There was a nest under the barn's eaves."

"I'm badly allergic to wasp stings," Abigail said. "So I made sure that the eaves were clear when I moved here. And I've had Randy check them periodically since then. Do you think Hoss could have...?"

"Had something to do with it? I doubt it. I think it was just an accident. I'll make sure to dispose of it today before the wasps do any more damage."

"It's a good thing you're such a good rider," Abigail said while mentally thinking, Geez, you need editing. Two *good*s in one sentence? Can't you do any better than that?

Luckily Dylan didn't seem to notice her repeated usage. "You know they say that man's best friend is a dog, but the Rom believe that a horse is a man's best friend. Traveler is special to me."

"Did the tobacco help?"

Dylan nodded.

"I've been meaning to ask you why my uncle had that round corral built over there," Abigail said.

"No corners where a horse can hide. Pete and I used to talk about training horses here at the ranch."

"You'd be good at that. You certainly have a way with animals."

"There ain't a horse that can't be rode..."

"And there ain't a man that can't be throwed," she continued, completing the rest of the well-known expression.

"The trick is in the hands," Dylan murmured, lightly running his fingers over her face, from the swirl of earlobe to the creamy curve of her cheek. "You've gotta use them to lavish attention."

Seeing the flare of confidence in his eyes only served to trigger her anger. Dylan was bedeviling her, an old-fashioned word, perhaps, but an accurate one. After two days of secretly watching him from her window, like some kind of lovesick voyeur, she was furious with herself...and with him, for being the cause of all her worry, angst, aggravation, anticipation.

Abigail had decided that she should have been able to resist his charms better. She also decided that she didn't appreciate him trying to charm her as if she were a mare. Whipping up her anger with a beater of righteous indignation, Abigail stepped away from his distracting touch to declare, "I'm not a horse you can tame with some sugar cubes, sweet words and lavish attention!"

"Sugar cubes will rot your horse's teeth," Dylan told her.

"I've had it! This has gone on long enough, I've had enough of your practicing your seduction skills on me."

"Seduction skills?" Dylan asked in amazement before making the dire mistake of letting his amusement show by laughing.

If there was one thing Abigail didn't take kindly to, it was being laughed at. It had happened to her once too often in her life—her parents laughing at her intention to take over her uncle's ranch, her peers' laughter at her plans of becoming a romance author, the last cowboy in her life laughing when she'd said she'd thought they'd had a future together.

By God, she was sick and tired of getting laughed at!

Seeing the fury spitting in her eyes, Dylan belatedly realized his error. "Now don't go getting all fired up about things...."

"Things?" she repeated, jabbing her finger at his chest. "We're not talking things here, cowboy! We're talking about respect. Respect for my opinions, for my feelings, for the fact that I want something you don't have. Security."

"A highly overrated commodity."

"In your opinion, not mine!"

"Now, honey..." he began, trying to placate her.

"You see?" she exclaimed. "That's what I mean. Stop patronizing me! You've never thought I knew anything about ranching, never given me credit for trying to do my best by this ranch. We managed for a month before you showed up. I did the same chores Shem and his sons are doing now. But do you acknowledge me as an equal? No. You're like my parents, acting like I'm a child and this ranch is some new toy that's caught my eye."

Unsure how to deal with Abbie in this kind of volatile mood, Dylan fell back on humor as a means of kidding her out of it. "You're no child, I'd be glad to testify to your parents on that account."

"You're not taking me seriously."

"Because you're being ridiculous. A little ridiculous," he amended. "All of this because I told you sugar rots your horse's teeth?"

Infuriated by his lack of understanding, Abigail was tempted to knock *his* teeth down his throat. "That does it. The chase stops here," Abigail declared, drawing a line in the dirt with her boot heel. "No more stolen little touches, no more serenading me with that damn guitar and no more kisses!"

"If you don't want me kissing you, you shouldn't kiss me back," he said in a voice he no doubt used on recalcitrant horses and stubborn children.

"Don't worry, I won't!"

"Won't what?"

"Kiss you back. Kiss you, period." Her curt words were like staccato gunshots. "This conversation is over."

As Abigail stomped back to the ranch house, Dylan turned to find the barn cat sitting on a nearby post. "Horses are easier to figure out than women."

The cat apparently was a female, because she stuck her nose in the air and haughtily jumped down and walked away. "You women always stick together," Dylan called after the cat.

Abigail got a lot of work done on the book in the next few days, but then she'd practically barricaded herself in her office since her fight with Dylan. She hadn't joined the others at mealtimes, instead grabbing a sandwich when the growling of her stomach became too much of a nuisance.

A knock on the door interrupted her editing of chapter nine. Raj tentatively poked her head around the door frame. "Is it okay to come in?"

Abigail nodded. "I could probably use a break about now," she admitted, rolling her head forward and lifting her shoulders up in an attempt to ease strained back muscles.

"This may be the best thing you've ever written," Raj said as she handed over the stack of pages she'd just read.

"You really think so?" Abigail asked uncertainly.

"You bet. This hero and heroine sure have some humdinger fights. That wouldn't have anything to do with the fact that you and Dylan aren't speaking at the moment, would it? What happened between you two?"

"I'd had it with his treating me as if I were some kind of bimbo."

"When did he do that?"

"He laughed at me."

"Oh-oh." Raj knew how sensitive Abigail was about that.

"I think it's just as well we cleared the air. Dylan and I have entirely different priorities. His priority is to get me into bed before he takes off. Mine is to finish this book."

"Ziggy stopped by for dinner tonight. Said he'd come tomorrow night, too. He was sorry you weren't joining us but said he understood your need to work. Then Shem talked about the muse, and Hondo thought it was some kind of intestinal problem."

As Abigail smiled, Raj said, "Ah, finally! I was wondering what I'd have to do to get a smile out of you."

"I'm sorry to be such a wet blanket," Abigail said.

"You're not a wet blanket. A slightly damp sheet, perhaps. But that's okay. You're a writer. You're entitled."

"Because I've got the muse, right?"

The two women cracked up.

Early the next morning, another sabotaging incident, even more serious than the others, brought Abigail back to earth. She went outside to drive the forty minutes into Big Rock and the post office when she found all four tires on her car had been slashed. This time, Abigail called the sheriff herself, insisting that he come out to take a look at the damage himself.

Shem felt badly because he'd been on night-watch duty when the incident occurred. "I'm no great prognosticator, but I should have seen something like this coming," Shem said, hanging his head and crunching his hat in his gnarled hands.

"You couldn't have known," Abigail reassured him. "I've already called the sheriff."

"He's not exactly known for his judicious judgment," Shem warned her.

"I didn't know Sheriff Tiber was Jewish," Hondo said. When his father smacked his arm with his hat, Hondo looked even more bewildered than usual. "What? What did I say this time?"

Sheriff Tiber didn't show up until almost six that evening, and then he only made a cursory inquiry at best.

"Teenagers," he said, spitting his chewing tobacco to one side of where they stood.

"Why would teenagers want to slash my car's tires? Unless someone put them up to it? Someone who wanted me off this ranch."

"And who might that be?"

"Hoss Redkins. I've told you before, he said I'd be sorry if I didn't sell to him."

"Of course you'd be sorry. He's made you a generous offer. That doesn't mean he'd arrange to have your tires slashed. Listen, I know that you've been away from town since you were a child, but I can tell you that he's an upstanding citizen of Big Rock. He casts a mighty big shadow in these parts."

Which put the unjudicious sheriff smack in the middle of Hoss's big shadow. Abigail was getting the picture now, and it wasn't a pretty one.

"This wouldn't have happened if Dawg was still alive," Hondo muttered over dinner that night.

Needing some company, and reminding herself that there was safety in numbers where her attraction to Dylan was concerned, Abigail had joined them around the scarred pine dining table that her uncle had made when she'd been just a little girl.

"Dawg was a good watchdog?" Raj asked.

Hondo nodded. "He was the best damn Chihuahua to ever bless this earth. For such a little dog, he had the biggest bark."

"That's what many women have said about me," Ziggy noted, making Raj and Abigail almost choke on their steaks.

Seeing the women's reaction, and wanting some attention himself, Hondo said, "Women say that about me, too."

"What about you, Dylan?" Randy challenged him. It was the first time he'd spoken during the meal, making Abigail wonder if he was holding a grudge against Dylan for that incident at the dance a few weeks back, when Dylan had refused to let him cut in on him. "What do women say about you?"

Seeing the two men together, it was only now occurring to her that Dylan was actually much younger than

Randy, probably by a good ten years at least. But Dylan was by far the more confident and mature of the two.

As if aware of her eyes on him, Dylan turned to face her. "You and I have to talk," he said quietly.

"No, we don't," she stated just as quietly.

"I asked you a question, Dylan," Randy reminded him with an angry edge to his voice.

"Maybe you should ask Abigail what women say about me," Dylan challenged.

Abigail couldn't be sure if he was challenging her or Randy or both of them.

"Women say Dylan is as inscrutable as the Great Sphinx," she replied.

Putting more mustard on his steak, Hondo said, "Are you saying Dylan smells? Because if you are, you should be around Hoss Redkins, the guy stinks like garlic all the time!"

Dylan knew he was in trouble with Abigail, and after dinner tonight he realized just how much trouble. She hadn't cooled down much since her temper tantrum in the barn a few days ago. It was time he called in reinforcements. So he called his dad.

"It is good you called. I have been having bad dreams," Konrad Janos told him. "They involve you."

"They're just dreams, Dad."

"Dreams are omens of things to come. Have you killed a ladybug or destroyed a robin nest?"

"Of course not. You raised me better. I know it's unlucky to kill a ladybug...."

"It is bad luck to destroy a robin nest, as well. To do so means that within the course of a year, you will break a bone."

"I've broken bones before, Dad. It kind of goes with the territory, you know."

"And I have never worried about your safety with your riding. Not until now."

"Have you been talking to Gaylynn?" Dylan asked suspiciously.

"You think I need to speak to your sister to know something is going on with you?"

"No."

"Good." Abruptly he said, "Tell me, which is greater, the dandelion or the oak?"

Accustomed to his father's ways, Dylan wasn't surprised by the abrupt change of subject. As he pondered the answer, he knew that the oak would be too obvious to be right, so he said, "The dandelion."

"Only if it has achieved the greatest fulfillment. A mature dandelion is greater than a stunted oak."

"Meaning what, Dad?"

"That you have yet to fulfill all your potentials. You remember what I told you about Roms having two successive lives? That God gave us the chance to live as we wanted, to make all the mistakes we could possibly make in our first life, and afterward make up for it in our second life?"

"Yeah, and you also told me that, unfortunately for me, this was my *second* life and that I was supposed to correct the mistakes I'd made in the first one." His dad laughed, clearly delighted that Dylan remembered this. "You'll be pleased to know that in this second life, I finally learned how to sing," Dylan added.

"It is the Rom box. Your sister has told me that there are secondary effects. I have seen them with your brother. You should see the way babies are drawn to him. Have you heard that he and Brett are thinking of starting a foster home? One that is done up right, Brett says.''

"I hadn't heard that."

"And so you have called your father because you are having trouble with love, yes?"

"I thought the Rom box was supposed to take care of all that."

"It brings you love, not peace."

"That's reassuring to know," Dylan grumbled.

"What is her name, this woman who has finally caught hold of my youngest son's heart?"

"Abigail."

His father repeated it, as if testing the sound of it. "It is an old-fashioned name, I think. Is she old-fashioned?"

"She's as stubborn as a mule."

"I am willing to bet she says the same about you, no?"

"She does."

Konrad chuckled. "Just remember that you cannot ride one saddle in two directions. In the old days, the Rom way would have been to kidnap the woman you wanted as your bride."

"Well, if I get desperate enough, I may end up having to do just that," Dylan joked.

But after he hung up, it did occur to Dylan that the old way might be the best way after all.

By the end of the week, Dylan had tried all the orthodox methods, tried talking to Abigail but he couldn't even get two minutes alone with her. She was bound and determined to avoid him, using her friends to keep him at bay. She clearly thought there was safety in a crowd. And Dylan had to admit that pouring out his heart in front of Ziggy or Shem was daunting, to say the least.

So he tried getting Raj on his side. *She,* at least, was still speaking to him.

Right after dinner, Abigail hightailed it off to that office of hers, mumbling something about being behind on her deadline. Dylan admired *her* behind as she sashayed out the door. Today she'd worn a white blouse and blue-and-white-flowered skirt. The denim vest she wore with it should have masked her breasts, but after feeling them brushing against him when they'd kissed, Dylan had developed X-ray vision and X-rated thoughts where she was concerned. More than once, he'd caught Abigail glancing over and, as if she'd been able to read his mind, glaring at him over a forkful of mashed potatoes.

"Raj, dinner tonight was really delicious," Dylan said as he picked up a plate and followed her into the kitchen.

"Clearing the table is woman's work," Randy called after him in warning.

Returning with Raj for another handful of plates, Dylan picked up Randy's plate. Seeing that Raj had returned to the kitchen, for a moment Dylan was tempted to dump the leftovers on Randy's lap, but the hired hand had practically licked his plate clean.

So Dylan had to make do with leaning closer to growl ominously, "Can the conversation or I'll have them serve you a big batch of fondue."

Randy took off like a bat out of hell, leaving Dylan alone with Raj. Knowing she was a rodeo fan, he began by sharing some amusing anecdotes about his life. Then, when she was softened up some, he said, "Maybe you could help me out with something."

"Sure, if I can."

"It's about Abbie..."

"Whoa, hold on right there. Abbie and I are friends—"

"I know that," he interrupted her. "And as her friend, I want you to talk to her."

"About?"

"About me."

"We've already talked about you."

"And?"

"You don't want to know," Raj assured him dryly.

"I know she's got this stupid thing about cowboys and not wanting to get involved...."

"It's more than a *thing*. She made a vow."

"A vow? You mean, like a nun or something?"

"Well, she's sworn to be celibate where cowboys are concerned."

Dylan tried not to panic. "So she's taken some falls in the past. That's no reason not to get back up on the horse again."

"It's not me you have to convince. It's Abbie."

"I would if I could talk to her for two minutes without an audience."

"I wouldn't hold your breath," Raj said. "Why are you so determined about this?"

"Damned if I know," Dylan muttered under his breath. All he knew was that he'd never felt this way before. He wanted Abbie more than he'd ever wanted a woman before. The wanting went home deep and it was threatening to take over his life. He *had* to have Abbie. Maybe then, he'd get his peace of mind back.

That didn't mean that Dylan was looking to get hitched or anything like that. *Long-term* wasn't a word in his vocabulary. But for the time he was here, he and Abbie could have some memorable times together—times that could last a man a long time. But he had to catch Abbie first.

"Listen," he told Raj, "I don't want you to be alarmed if I should do something . . . something in regard to Abbie that might be a little outrageous."

"Care to fill me in ahead of time?"

"No. That way you won't have to lie and say you knew what was going on."

"For what it's worth, I've told her that I think you're worth taking a risk on."

With a confident grin, Dylan assured her, "I'm worth a lot more than that. And I aim on convincing Abbie of that!"

Gypsy kidnappings were perhaps best done at midnight, but the reality was that riding in the dark was hard enough without a struggling female in his arms, one that he found distracting as all get-out. So he had to snatch her in broad daylight.

Dylan made his plans carefully. He left a note for Raj, telling her that he'd taken Abbie up to an old homesteader's cabin in the high country in a far corner of the property, knowing that neither she nor anyone else at the ranch would be able to find it, and that they'd be back in a few days.

So he tracked Abigail down taking an afternoon stroll to her favorite place, the hillside directly behind the ranch house. She liked sitting at the top beside the two tall fir trees standing sentinel up there, and had even created a perch of sorts on a fence rail. Dylan had Traveler pick his way carefully among the quivering aspen groves below.

Dylan decided to approach Abigail from the front, rather than sneaking up on her from behind. She was wearing jeans and a red shirt. Dylan grinned. Knowing that red was a lucky color in love, he'd worn a red bandanna himself.

She looked surprised to see him. She looked even more surprised when he leaned over and scooped her into his arms and onto the back of his horse.

What do you think you're doing?" she shrieked.

"Kidnapping you. So sit back and enjoy it."

Seven

———

"**A**re you crazy?" Abigail turned her head to shout, only to have her long hair blow into her mouth. Spitting it out while making growling noises of frustration, she went on to yell, "Have you been drinking? If you think this is some kind of joke, I am *not* amused!"

"The amusement comes later," Dylan assured her with a devilish grin before tightening his arms around her waist. "Don't get any wild ideas about getting free," he warned her. "One of us could break our necks."

That sounded threatening. Which left Abigail wondering if she'd been had. Had she been looking to Hoss Redkins as the source of all the trouble she'd had, when Dylan was really to blame? Or had Dylan done Hoss's dirty work for him, and the ensuing arguments between them just been a smoke screen for her benefit? Abigail didn't know what to think anymore.

"Where are you taking me?" she demanded.

"On a tour of your property," he replied.

"I suppose it wouldn't do me any good to tell you that I don't want to take a tour of my property with you."

"I know you're angry with me at the moment," he began.

"Try furious!" she interrupted him.

"But I didn't have any choice. You wouldn't talk to me at the ranch, so I had to find a way for us to get away. If you hadn't been so stubborn . . ."

"Me? You're the one who could give a mule lessons!" She added a disapproving sniff for good measure.

Dylan's horse, Traveler, carried them both with good-natured ease, the pace a steady one. Dylan was encouraged by the fact that Abigail hadn't taken it into her mind to try to escape. But he could practically hear the gears spinning in that mind of hers.

"What are you thinking about?" he asked her.

"You don't want to know."

"If I didn't want to know, I wouldn't have asked you."

"I'm wondering what you hope to gain by this ridiculous action."

"You're thinking more than that," he said.

"Oh, so now you know what I'm thinking better than I do? Talk about the ultimate egotist."

"You're not scared, are you?"

"Of course not," she scoffed.

But he felt the slight tremor that went through her.

"You know I wouldn't hurt you for the world."

"Yeah, you and Hoss Redkins both."

Dylan stiffened. "Redkins and I have nothing in common."

"You're both bullies who think they can do whatever they want."

"You know what I want?" Dylan whispered as he nuzzled the sensitive skin behind her ear.

"This ranch," she retorted.

"Where did that come from? You think this is about the *ranch?*"

"Isn't it?"

"Hell no!"

"Then what is this about?"

"This," he said right before turning her face toward his to kiss her.

You'd have thought she'd be used to his kisses by now—she thought she'd experienced the full spectrum, from teasing to hot. But once again, Dylan caught her by surprise.

This kiss was unlike the others. It was more. More direct, more passionate, more forceful.

Luckily Traveler was well trained enough to manage navigating on his own while his riders were temporarily distracted.

Abigail had no idea how long Dylan's mouth remained on hers. Decades could have gone by, and she wouldn't have known it. All she knew was that her lips were clinging to his with wanton acceptance. His arms were all that was keeping her upright.

When Dylan finally raised his head, he also raised his hand, from her waist to cup her breast. "Your heart is pounding."

"So is yours," she whispered. "Holy buffalo chips!"

"That good or bad?"

Dylan was both. He looked *soooo* good, the red bandanna he wore around his neck merely accenting his Gypsy heritage, evident in his high cheekbones and fiery dark eyes.

"Ah, we're here," he said, not waiting for an answer.

Here turned out to be a tiny cabin.

"It's an old homesteader's cabin," Dylan said.

Having belatedly recovered some of her missing composure, she retorted, "Is that meant to make me like it?"

"I thought you liked the history of the West."

"I do. I don't like being kidnapped on horseback."

"No? You've had it in two of your books."

Instead of answering, Abigail focused on dismounting from his horse with as much finesse as possible.

When Dylan had first grabbed her, she'd been ready to murder him. Now she wasn't so sure. Riding double, sitting in the V of his thighs for two hours, had turned her backbone to mush. He'd kissed every smidge of her strawberry Chap Stick from her lips, and she was getting a sunburn on her nose.

"Okay, you got me up here, now what did you want to talk to me about?" she demanded, complete with an impatient tap of her booted foot.

"What's the hurry?" Dylan countered, absently rubbing his injured leg. "We've got time."

"I don't. In case you hadn't noticed, I'm on deadline."

"You're ahead of schedule, thanks to all the hours you've put in at the keyboard the past few days. Besides, those wrists of yours need a break. You don't want to get carpal tunnel syndrome, do you?"

"How do you know about carpal tunnel?" she demanded. "Have you been talking to Raj? You have, haven't you! Was she in on this plan?"

"No way. She's your friend. She'd never betray your friendship."

"She's a friend with a weakness for cowboys," Abigail retorted. "All you'd have to do is dazzle her with some rodeo talk and smile at her..."

"You think I can dazzle, huh? That's nice to know."

"You can be charming when you want to be. Heck, you could probably convince a polar bear to buy ice, but that doesn't mean anything you say is more than just hot air. And I'm not wild about outhouses, either," she added with a pointed look at the recognizable structure out back.

"A country girl like you should be used to roughing it now and again. Unless you've gotten too citified down in Great Falls?"

"Oh, no, I'm not falling into that trap. You think all you have to do is throw out a challenge and I'll pick up the gauntlet . . . What are you doing?"

"What does it look like I'm doing? I'm taking off my shirt."

"I can see that. Why are you taking off your shirt? Certainly not for my benefit, I hope."

"Why, how could taking off my shirt benefit you?" he asked with feigned innocence, undoing another three buttons.

"It couldn't," she maintained, swallowing.

"Your tongue is hanging out," he teased her. "Not that it's not an adorable tongue," he added. "Velvet soft and sweeter than wild strawberries."

She couldn't get her tongue to work anymore, to form words. It was glued to the roof of her mouth—the part that wasn't hanging out, that is.

"It *is* warm out here, isn't it?" he noted with a smile.

She was just about burning up.

"You ever gone skinny-dipping before?"

"When I was about eight, maybe."

"Then it's time you did it again. There's a river right over there with a pool deep enough to swim in."

"And freeze your bottom off in."

Dylan just smiled and shrugged, drawing her attention to his shoulders. He didn't have an extra ounce of fat on him. In fact, he was so lean he was borderline skinny.

Thinking of him as skinny somehow made her feel better. That is, until he reached for the buckle on his belt and the top metal rivet on his jeans.

"You blushing, or is it that darn sunburn again?" Dylan teased her.

Something in Abigail rebelled. She'd had enough of playing the victim here. It was time she gave Dylan a taste of his own medicine.

"Okay, cowboy, you want to go skinny-dipping? Fine." Reaching up, she pulled an elastic band from her jeans pocket and redid her hair so that it was piled on top of her head. "We'll go skinny-dipping. And we'll see who is blushing."

Now it was his turn to ask "What are you doing?" as she shifted her attention from her hair to the buttons of her shirt, making short work of them.

"What does it look like I'm doing?" she mockingly retorted, throwing his own words back at him... along with her red shirt. "I'm taking off my shirt."

Beneath it, she wore a cotton chemise that made a tank top look like a suit of armor. Dylan saw that, once he'd unwrapped her shirt from his face. The sleeves had wrapped around his neck like a clinging lover.

"What's the matter, cowboy?" Abigail taunted him. "You can dish it out, but you can't take it?"

"I can take it just fine," Dylan maintained, his voice regaining that desperado edge to it—hot and dusty and a little dangerous. A little breathless, too? she wondered.

"I believe the next move is yours," she told him, folding her arms and tapping her booted foot.

Dylan shook his head in disbelief. "You're something else, do you know that?"

"Getting cold feet?"

"Honey, there isn't one inch of me that's cold. Care to test that claim yourself?"

"Nope."

He grinned at her laconic reply. "Your loss."

"Are you going to stand there talking all day or are you going to go skinny-dipping?"

Dylan tugged off his boots, first his right and then his left.

Abigail did the same.

"Ladies first," Dylan drawled with a nod at her jeans.

Telling herself that she wouldn't be displaying anything that couldn't be seen in a two-piece swimsuit, Abigail undid the zipper on her jeans and shimmied them down her hips. She could have sworn she heard Dylan groan.

Looking up through her lashes, she saw the startled expression on his face. So, he hadn't thought she'd do it. Deciding to make the most of the moment, she took her time removing her jeans, running her hands first down her right leg to remove the denim covering and then her left.

All the while, Dylan was practically eating her up with his eyes.

When the jeans were finally off, she took great pleasure in tossing them right at him.

He caught them one-handed, his eyes remaining glued to her legs.

The briefs she wore were durable white cotton, nothing out of a lingerie catalog. But you wouldn't know that by the way Dylan was staring at her.

"Cat got your tongue, cowboy?" she inquired.

He licked his lips as if he could practically taste her.

"Not that it isn't an adorable tongue," she saucily added, once again tossing his own words back at him.

"Enough," he growled.

"I don't think so. You're still wearing your jeans."

Two seconds later, they were gone. His underwear was also white, the bulging front placket indicating his fully aroused state.

"Looks like you could use a dip in cold water," she tossed over her shoulder before darting past him to get into the river.

"Cute, very cute," he said.

"Yes, you are," she retorted, using the palm of her hand to splash water at him as he stood on the riverbank.

"You're asking for it," he warned her.

"Absolutely not. I'm merely trying to make the best of a...rank situation."

"Rank, huh? Saddle-bronc riders really look forward to rank rides, you know. Have you been brushing up on your rodeo terms? You've got try, I'll give you that."

A *rank* ride was one with plenty of fireworks, and *try* was guts and determination. "So do you," she returned, trying not to ogle him too obviously as he moseyed on into the water.

She moved backward, nearly falling over in her haste to keep a certain amount of distance between them. The fact that the pool was only about fifteen feet across limited her retreat. The water was cold but not frigid, having been warmed by the sun in this elbow of the river.

She was warmed by his nearness. He'd kept on his briefs, thank heavens. Seconds later, her eyes widened as he tossed his wet underwear back toward the shore. "Ah, that's better," he noted. "Don't you think?"

She couldn't think. Not coherently, anyway. All she could do was imagine, and drool as she watched the droplets of water gleaming on his shoulders and chest. She clenched her hands to prevent herself from reaching out and following the path of each individual drop from his collarbone down his chest, to his navel.

Moments later, he dived under the water, only to reappear right beside her. His long dark hair hung in wet strands. When he shook his head, he splattered her with water.

His grin flashed like summer lightning, echoing the thunder of her heart. "Enjoying your kidnapping so far?"

She slapped water smack in his face.

In retaliation, he dunked her. And when he let her go, he dived under the water again, this time to snap the elastic waistband of her underwear. The man had no decency! No modesty, either.

"Okay, that does it," she growled. "This is war!"

They cavorted like a couple of kids until the water got too cold. She got out of the water first and busied herself getting dried off, using her shirt as a towel, while he got out.

In the end, Abigail couldn't resist taking a peek at him while he was standing there, dripping wet and stark naked.

"Girls go nuts for cowboy butts," she murmured under her breath.

"What did you say?"

"That we were nuts to stay in the water so long. It's cold."

"I can warm you up," Dylan offered, ambling closer.

Picking up his hat, she shoved it at his naked body, covering his private parts. "You just stay right where you are."

"For how long?"

"Until you're decent."

"Well, now, ma'am," he drawled, "that might take a while because I've been called many things, but decent ain't necessarily one of them."

"Very funny."

Actually Abigail had to reluctantly admit that Dylan really had been pretty decent to her, offering his help when he saw she needed it on the ranch. Heaven knew that the wages she offered weren't all that good. But he'd agreed to stay out of a loyalty to her uncle. And that said a lot about Dylan. He was capable of strong feelings—of loyalty, anyway.

"I know what we need to warm up," he noted as he headed for his saddlebags and some fresh clothes.

"I can imagine," she said, eyeing his naked bottom until he glanced over his shoulder and shifted his hat there. His telltale grin made her blush.

"I was talking about starting a fire."

She was already on fire.

"You got any objections to that?"

Abigail didn't think she had the energy left to object to anything. She shook her head. She was tempted to object when he got dressed, it seemed a shame to cover that body with clothes.

That *skinny* body, she tried to remind herself . . . to no avail. No, he wasn't skinny, he was lean and muscular and just right.

Flustered, Abigail tried to distract herself by focusing on her surroundings. She hadn't been up here in ages. The cabin had been built by her great-grandfather who'd come to Montana from the plains of Kansas in 1890. Her roots went deep into this land.

As if reading her mind, Dylan said, "It's beautiful country."

Abigail nodded, her hair tilting a little and making her look even more endearing in Dylan's view.

"Family legend has it that my great-granddad picked this location because it was close to water and game," she said with a reminiscent smile. "But the women in my family always claimed that the real truth was that he picked this place because my great-grandmother saw it and said that this was as close to heaven as she cared to get until she reached sixty or so. She lived to be seventy-eight and never did leave this property. That probably seems strange to a man like you, someone who travels all the time and is always hitting the open road. But she'd found what she was looking for, and was smart enough to know it."

"I can see where a view like this might tempt a person to stay," Dylan murmured.

Abigail raised her face to the sunshine, which felt warmer here in the higher elevation. The air was filled with the scent of pine. The *rat-a-tat-tat* sound of a woodpecker at work reminded her of her last New Year's resolution to learn more about the birds in her home state. It was something she'd been meaning to do...just as she'd meant to visit the cabin once she'd finished her deadline and had more time on her hands. Her hands...what she really wanted on her hands was Dylan.

Great! Why did all her thoughts lead back to him?

"Getting hungry?" Dylan asked her.

"Starved," she murmured, her gaze drawn to his sensual mouth and those beautiful male lips that Michelangelo couldn't have sculpted any better.

"I've got something for you, then," he said.

"Mmm?" she replied, distracted by the way his lips pursed when he said *you*.

"Dinner." He triumphantly held up a small plastic cooler that he'd retrieved from the river. "Cold chicken and the fixings."

"Sounds like you raided the fridge when Raj wasn't looking."

"Guilty as charged."

Noticing the way she was rubbing her hands up and down her arms, Dylan said, "It's getting cool out here. We better go on inside and get that fire going that I promised you."

While Dylan did that, Abigail set the unsteady table, sticking a folded, empty matchbook under one leg to help keep it stabilized. She added a small handful of summer wildflowers to an empty mason jar she found on the shelf beside the window.

The same window her great-grandmother must have looked out of. She found herself imagining what it must have been like for her great-grandmother, coming from the vast flatness of the plains to the valleys and rugged mountains of northwestern Montana. The view suddenly turned fuzzy as bellows of smoke rolled across the cabin from the fireplace.

Dylan grabbed her elbow and together they ran outside, coughing and eyes watering.

Abigail was the first to speak. "And here I was, thinking you were an expert at starting fires," she noted mockingly.

"*Starting* them, not controlling them," Dylan countered, feeling like a green-as-grass tenderfoot for not checking the chimney to make sure it was clear and no birds had set up housekeeping in it before he started a fire. He'd tried to plan ahead and had even cleaned up the cabin some before bringing her up here.

"You look like a hoot owl with all that soot on your face," she said, laughter making her voice quiver. Since he'd been squatting right in front of the fireplace, he'd gotten a faceful.

"Oh, yeah? Wanna see how owls kiss?" Swooping down, he rubbed his nose against hers before nuzzling her cheek, making strange, supposedly owl-like noises. She was giggling so hard she couldn't even speak. She'd laughed more with Dylan than she had with anyone.

"Mmm, you smell like *eau de charcoal,*" Dylan murmured in between smacking kisses to her neck.

"I love a man who speaks French," she murmured in reply before it hit her. She *did* love Dylan.

Shaken by the self-discovery, she stepped away from his teasing embrace to say, "Now what?"

Her question could just as well have applied to herself—what was she going to do now that she knew she'd fallen in love with Dylan? There was no fighting it; it was too late for that. Maybe the time had come to accept it, to hug the knowledge like a cherished heirloom.

"Now what?" Dylan repeated. "First off, I clean up down at the river and then we eat out here. Let the cabin air out some."

So, instead of sitting at the table with the wildflowers she'd picked, they sat around a camp fire, munching on cold chicken and drinking hot coffee while swapping tall tales of the old West.

"You mean to tell me you never heard of the Good-night-Loving Trail?" Dylan asked in amazement, sliding an arm around her shoulders, ostensibly to keep the blanket they were sharing in place. "Why, I find that hard to believe."

"I believe you're making the entire thing up," she countered.

"Charles Goodnight and Oliver Loving wouldn't thank you for saying that. They forged the Goodnight-Loving Trail from Texas to Kansas."

Abigail got to thinking about Dylan forging a good-night-loving trail from her temple to her thigh.

"Goodnight is credited with inventing the chuck wagon. I would have thought you'd know that, what with your interest in the old West and all."

She probably did know that, but the problem was that her interest at the moment was almost one hundred percent focused on Dylan—on the rise and fall of his chest as he breathed, on the way she could feel each of his fingers as they gently held the rounded curve of her shoulder. Dylan was emanating as much warmth as the fire, if not more!

Feeling herself slipping badly, Abigail tried to keep her thoughts on the high road. "Mary Easterly," she gasped, as if grasping at straws. "Now, she had quite a story. A real, honest-to-goodness cattle queen, only of Nevada not Montana. She didn't have a large herd, but it was prime. Because she prided herself on quality not quantity."

"So do I. Pride myself on quality." His hand had somehow edged up her shoulder so that he could graze her earlobe with his caressing thumb. "And that's something you've got plenty of, Abbie. Quality. Class."

Feeling her backbone melting, Abigail searched desperately around for something to say. "So tell me how a Chicago boy like you ended up out west. I thought most rodeo cowboys grew up on ranches."

"I grew up on the back of a horse," Dylan replied, continuing his strangely reassuring yet sublimely seductive caress of her ear. "On the weekends anyway. I've always been good around horses. My dad put me on the back of one when I was three and we visited the Illinois State Fair in Springfield, and I haven't been off much since then."

"There aren't many horses in the city."

"No, but there are some stables out near the Cook County Forest Preserves. By the time I was fifteen, I was working in one of them all summer. The next two summers, I went up to Wisconsin and spent two months on a horse farm up there. Those were racing horses, polo horses, thoroughbreds. High-strung." His glance said *Like you,* but he was wise enough not to actually say the words out loud. "I was good with them."

"I'm sure you were," she muttered.

"But I was better with the horses that couldn't be rode. The wild ones. Anyway, after I graduated from high school, I came out west, went to rodeo school in southern Idaho and I've been out here ever since."

"What made you choose rodeo?"

"I'm good at it. I mean, I *was* good at it."

"You never worried about getting hurt?"

"In rodeo, it's not a matter of *when* you'll get hurt, just how badly."

"Gee, that would sure make me want to try it," she retorted in exasperation.

"You say you grew up out here. Rodeoing is a part of life here, you know that. There aren't many things a man can do and be his own boss and keep his freedom with no one telling him what to do. I rode nearly a hundred horses last year. Some of them rank, some of them not. You know what they say... that riding a saddle bronc is kind of like playing the guitar. It's mighty easy to do it poorly and mighty hard to do it well."

"Did you pick up riding as fast as you did the guitar?"

Dylan shrugged. "It just sort of always came naturally to me. There's just no feeling like it, that moment when the chute opens and it's just me and the horse."

"You were there by choice, the horse wasn't."

"Most people don't have any use for a horse that bucks. Those horses would have been put down if they weren't used in rodeo."

"And what about the arenas filled with fans? Didn't that have something to do with your love for rodeo?"

"No. For those eight seconds, all you're trying to do is stay on that twisting, bucking horse. It rears up and slams you back down again, so hard you think your brains have hit the roof of your head. The horse's hoofs are punching the dust, threatening to pulverize you into the dirt ten feet below, and nothing else matters. The adrenaline is pumping, and you're just focusing on staying on."

Abigail shuddered. She'd attended a few rodeos, but it wasn't her favorite way of spending time. She'd always worried too much about one of the contestants or one of the animals getting hurt. "Wasn't there anything about rodeo that you didn't like?"

"The commute. I put nearly a hundred thousand miles on my truck last year. Rodeo is a year-long event. In the winter, the competitions are mostly inside stadiums in places like Denver. In spring and summer, things heat up and rodeos move on outside. Practically every day, one town or another has a rodeo going. I always had good luck in Pocatello, Idaho, at the National Circuit Finals there. And the Calgary Stampede in July... that's just about as close to rodeo heaven as you can come. Prize money is pretty spectacular, too. Now, some folks prefer Cheyenne, the 'daddy of 'em all,' but not me. And it all leads to the NFR in Las Vegas in December."

"Raj and I saw that movie, *Eight Seconds,* about the bull rider who was killed riding in the Cheyenne rodeo."

"That was a freak accident. I can give you the statistics of how few men have been killed..."

"And I'm willing to bet they don't keep statistics on how many are injured."

"Heck, no. Every rider has gashes, sprains and bruises by Labor Day."

"And how many men are permanently injured?"

Dylan shifted uncomfortably, momentarily halting his soothing touch. "How did we get on this subject anyway?"

"I was trying to figure out why you'd want to get hurt."

"I don't want to, it's just part of life. Which reminds me, I hope you know that I would never do anything to hurt you. I know you were kind of scared earlier...."

"I was not!" she immediately denied.

"But I'd never hurt you." He looked directly into her eyes as he spoke the words.

"I thought being hurt was a part of life," she countered unsteadily.

"It's not the only part of life. Pleasure is another, bigger part of life." He moved his hand so that the warmth of his palm now cupped her nape. Urging her forward, he whispered against her lips, "I think we should go inside now . . . for dessert. I've got something special for you."

She imagined him wearing a wicked smile and nothing else. Mmm, yes, that sure would qualify as something special in her book. She wasn't imagining strawberries.

Dylan fed the first one to her chastely enough. It wasn't her fault the fruit was so ripe and juicy that it dripped from her lips. She laughed self-consciously as she attempted to wipe the juice away with her fingers.

"Let me," Dylan said. Only, he didn't use his fingers for the cleanup; he used his seductive tongue, lapping at her skin as if she were a huge bowl of cream and he a hungry tomcat.

But he didn't kiss her. Instead, he leaned away to get another strawberry. This time, he took a bite out of it first. Then he held the juicy fruit up to her lips, tracing their circumference, coloring her lower lip and outlining her upper lip with the red juice.

And all the while, he was staring at her mouth as if it were the most fascinating, intoxicating thing he'd ever seen in his entire life.

Ripples of anticipation shivered up Abigail's spine. She almost forgot to breathe.

Sensual tension. She'd written pages and pages about it. But she'd never felt it before, never experienced it so fully that she could almost reach out and touch it in the air. The space between herself and Dylan hummed with it, was thick with it.

The talk about his life chasing rodeo had only reinforced her fears about the life he'd led in the past, and the fact that she'd fallen in love with him now. She knew where this night was leading. She felt poised on the head of a pin, trying to make the right move to avoid falling on her face.

"You seem to have planned ahead," she noted, indicating the quilt on the bed and the fresh pillows. She'd even found a couple of rolls of toilet paper in the outhouse.

"Yeah, I did, except for the chimney. I brought some things up here this morning."

"How long have you been planning this kidnapping?"

"Hey, I'll have you know that kidnapping a bride is a time-honored Gypsy tradition."

BRIDE? Abigail heard the word all in capital letters, and her hopes took flight. Could she have been wrong about Dylan? She must have been. He'd called her a bride. That meant she must have been wrong about Dylan. After being footloose for so long, he *was* looking for the same thing she was. Some permanence. Some love. Some stability.

Her doubts were smothered beneath the tidal wave of relief that her dreams were coming true. All her senses were turned up to their highest pitch, tuned in to the smallest sound. Candlelight flickered on his skin and hers, creating a golden glow that mirrored her emotions. They were serenaded by the sounds of nature: the soft music created by the rushing river behind the cabin, the rustle of the leaves as the night wind moved them with fluid grace. Inside the cabin, there was only a hint of smoke in the air, an aftereffect from Dylan's earlier attempts at building a fire.

The fire he was building now was an erotic one. Flames leapt from every point of contact with Dylan—the brush of his denim-clad thigh against her, his open mouth nuzzling against her collarbone, his nimble fingers tugging her red shirt from the waistband of her jeans.

At first, there was no sense of urgency, but rather of anticipation, of wanting to enjoy every second along the way rather than rushing it. So she paused to taste the curve of his jaw, sampling the salty roughness with her tongue.

When his roughened fingertips drifted up the valley of her spine, she arched her back in delicious pleasure. Her movement thrust her breasts against his chest.

Suddenly his caresses took on a new heat. His lips met hers, parting them with sweet insistence. He feasted on her, luring her toward the point of no return. The kiss was a fervent seduction of her senses, a mating of lips and swirling tongues.

Abigail was burning up, so she welcomed the fact that Dylan removed her shirt. She returned the favor by removing his. The quilt on the bed was rumpled within seconds of them lying on it.

Her jeans were tossed over the end of the bed, soon to be joined by his. Now the pace intensified. Being horizontal with him was infinitely better than vertical, she decided with a moan of pleasure. Now she was pressed against every inch of his lean body, which was hard in all the right places.

"Abbie," he whispered, dispensing a string of kisses from the corner of her eyes to the hollow of her breast. "I'm giving you a choice." His hands paused on the front of her chemise. "If this goes further, it's your decision."

She combed her hands through his glorious midnight-dark hair, just as she'd so often longed to do, and marveled at the sensation of the vibrant coolness against her fingers.

"Yes or no," he said huskily. "It's in your hands."

"It's not in my hands yet, cowboy," she drawled with a sultry smile. "But it will be soon." Rolling him over so that she sat propped on his chest, she slid her hands past his navel before sneaking beneath the waistband of his briefs. Tracing the throbbing velvety length of his arousal, she whispered, "The answer is yes."

Groaning and lifting his hips at the dark magic she was practicing on him, Dylan growled out his promise for the ride of her life.

"I'll bet you tell all the girls that," she murmured against his thigh.

Threading his fingers through her hair, he raised her head so that he could look in her glorious blue eyes. "You're one of a kind."

"Your first time with an older woman?" she teased in an attempt to hide her sudden nervousness.

"My first time with someone who means this much to me."

"How much do I mean to you?"

"Let me show you."

And he did, with every stroke of his tongue over the hidden secrets of her body. As the waves of ecstasy rolled over her, he cupped her feminine mound with the palm of his hand, as if to cherish the moment.

"Now," she whispered. "I want you inside of me."

After taking care of protection, he levered himself into readiness before coming to her in gratifying increments, prolonging the ultimate delight, rubbing against her with excruciating sureness, easing deeper and deeper.

"You like it slow?" he whispered. "Like this?"

"Yes!" She clenched her fingers into his shoulders and gasped his name.

"Good."

"Very good," she agreed breathlessly. "More."

"More of this?" He rocked against her.

"Yes!"

"Or this?" He surged against her.

"*Yes!*" She lifted her hips to meet his rhythmic thrust.

"Abbie! Honey, I can't hold on . . . we're gonna gallop to the finish here. . . ."

"Galloping . . . is . . . good," she gasped. She watched the fire in his dark eyes as passion took hold, of her and him. The pleasure was becoming so intense that she couldn't think anymore, just feel.

When Dylan reached down to brush his roughened thumb against the burgeoning nub hidden deep in the thicket of blond curls, she immediately went up in spirals of smoke, rising upward with each blissfully sharp pulse of pure joy—tightening and rippling, tightening and rippling.

Feeling her tightening around him as she reached her climax made Dylan feel like a million bucks, as if he'd touched a part of heaven. He struggled to maintain control, but there was no holding out against the flare of desire surging through him. Shouting her name, he drove into her for one final time before arching his back and stiffening as he reached his completion.

Afterward, with her head resting on his shoulder as they lay together in the small bed with the quilt wrapped around their entwined bodies, Abigail propped herself up on one hand to look down at Dylan. "What are you thinking about?" she asked, unable to resist running her fingertip across his bare chest while tracing out an invisible heart with his initials and hers.

"Branding me, are you?" Dylan inquired, a grin flashing across his face like summer heat lightning.

"You ever been branded before?"

"No, but I've been stomped on a few times."

Her expression turned serious. She'd felt the scar across his right thigh. It scared her to think of how easily he could have been lost to her.

With that realization came the need to make love with him again, to reaffirm the fact that they were both alive. "How many condoms did you bring with you?"

His grin turned into a downright wicked smile as he murmured, "Enough."

Rolling so that she was perched atop him, she said, "Good."

"Are you going to practice that scene from *Flame of the West*?" he asked with unconcealed anticipation.

She nodded, her long blond hair trailing over his skin like curled ribbons of silk. "My heroine, Loretta, was better endowed than I am, though," she noted with a frown.

"No way," Dylan denied, cupping her breasts in his palms, one in each hand. "Look how well they fit," he noted, gently rubbing the rosy tips with his thumbs. "The first time I met you, I knew I was in trouble. I always knew you'd be handful," he added wickedly.

"Mmm, I could say the same about you," she replied, scooting down his torso to curl her hand around his throbbing maleness. "More than a handful."

This time, she was the one who got the latex condom open and sheathed him with it. Then, with her bent knees bracketing his hips, she slowly guided him to her. Once he was ensconced deep within her, he showed her just how to increase the pleasure. The embers of passion quickly flared.

Suddenly sitting up, Abigail found herself perched in his lap with Dylan facing her instead of lying beneath her.

Blinking in surprise, her mouth formed a startled *O* which Dylan took great pleasure in kissing from her lips.

"You ever ridden the teeter-totter as a kid?" he murmured against her lips.

She nodded.

"You just lean forward and back."

He watched her face as she concentrated on moving as he'd said and then witnessed her second blink of surprise as she succeeded. "Oh, my!"

"Mmm," Dylan agreed, taking his turn leaning back as she moved forward.

"How long does this last?"

"Longer than eight seconds, less than eight hours," he said with a devilish smile.

"Show me."

He did.

Rosy sunlight heralding the dawn was filtering through the wavy leaded-glass windows when Abigail next opened her eyes. For a second, she had no idea where she was, except that she was in Dylan's arms. She knew that. Recognized the uniqueness of his touch. They were lying spoon fashion, cuddled together for warmth, since Dylan never had gotten around to clearing out the chimney to build a fire there. Instead, he'd spent the night building fires within her.

She slowly stretched. Her movement woke Dylan, who blinked sleepily at her before smiling. She thought she'd never seen anything so beautiful in her life. This was the definition of happiness. Waking up in Dylan's arms, watching him smile at her.

"So do you want a small wedding or a large one?" she asked.

The words were no sooner out of her mouth than Dylan stiffened, panic and disbelief stamped on his face.

And that's when it hit her—despite the night they'd spent together and the lovemaking they'd shared, Dylan did not plan on having her as his bride.

Eight

"I was kidding," Abigail immediately declared, even as she scurried out of his arms like a startled water bug. "Can't you take a joke? I mean really, you and I permanently? We'd kill each other."

"Yeah, but what a way to go," Dylan murmured.

"Right." She tugged on her clothes.

"Where are you going?" he demanded.

"Outside," she said.

"Why?"

"Mother Nature calls."

"Oh. Hurry on back."

Once outside, instead of visiting the outhouse, Abigail took the time to try to regain her shattered control. What an idiot she'd been.

Inhaling lungfuls of crisp air, she wondered how she could have been so naive as to think that Dylan was ready for marriage. She'd heard the word *bride* and gone weak

at the knees. Her brains and reasoning powers had turned
to red Montana dust.

The sunrise was spectacular as a calm splendor spread
over the mountains, softening their edges, turning the sky
into a rosy wash of color. But Abigail couldn't appreciate it. This was a land of extremes. And her own feelings
were equally extreme.

The reason this hurt so much was that she'd gone and
done the inevitable and the foolish deed of falling in love
with Dylan Janos.

She'd taken every precaution; she really had. But despite her eloquent and frequently delivered self-warnings,
in the end she hadn't been able to get her heart to agree
with her head. Her head knew better than to get involved with a rolling stone like Dylan—a man who never
looked more than a few weeks ahead, a man who didn't
include the words *future* or *stability* in his vocabulary.

But her heart...ah, her heart had seen his flashing dark
eyes and his incredible lips. Had it stopped there, she
could attribute this aching pain to humiliation, and her
feelings for Dylan as nothing more than physical attraction.

But there was more to Dylan than lips or eyes or even
a cowboy butt. There was his dry sense of humor, his
willingness to help others, the kindness with which he
treated animals, from horses to the barn cat who wanted
nothing to do with humans. Dylan had convinced the fe-
line otherwise. Just as he'd convinced Abigail that there
had been a chance that he'd been serious, that he *really*
had kidnapped her to be his bride.

But he hadn't meant that reference to kidnapping a
bride to be taken seriously. He didn't see her as his bride.
That much had been clear from the stark panic and disbelief on his face when she'd talked about a wedding.

She had to act like an adult about this. She didn't want him knowing how stupid she'd been. Humiliation blended with her bone-deep pain. But she couldn't just stand out here, blinking back tears like a kid who'd just found out that Santa didn't exist. She had to go back inside, or Dylan would start getting suspicious. She didn't want him questioning her behavior.

"You were gone a long time," Dylan noted as she walked in the front door. "I missed you."

"It's getting cold out at night. Autumn is just around the corner. Might come early this year."

Which would mean that Dylan would leave early, she silently noted.

"I know how to warm you back up," Dylan murmured, turning back the cover on the bed invitingly.

When she didn't react, he said, "What's wrong?"

"Nothing."

Dylan sighed. "Look, about what I said earlier..."

"Don't worry about it," she dismissed curtly. "We're both adults. Let's not make more of what happened here than really did. We both enjoyed ourselves. Let's just leave it at that. You're not the type of man I'm looking for anyway," she stated.

It was one thing for Dylan to think that he wasn't ready to settle down, but it was something else again for her to say it, to say he wasn't the type of man for her. Or was she saying that she wasn't in the market for a banged-up, ex-rodeo saddle-bronc rider? He was hardly what you'd call a catch. Sure, he'd done all right, even investing part of his money instead of blowing it on the high life, but she was a famous author, making damn good money. To her, he must seem like a saddle bum.

"So last night was just the boss lady rolling in the hay with the hired help, is that it?" he growled.

"Listen, you've got no call to be acting insulted," Abigail retorted angrily. "I'm the one who..."

"Yes? The one who what?"

"Who is not riding back on that horse with you," she declared, stopping herself in time from disclosing her true feelings, the love she felt for him. Unrequited love. "When you get down to the ranch house, have Shem or one of his sons bring Wild Thing up here. Until then, I'll stay here."

"Forget it."

"You may have gotten your way before, but you aren't again," she vowed fiercely.

"We'll see about that. Meanwhile, you can ride Traveler down. I'll wait here. Randy and I needed to check out the fencing on the property line up here anyway. Send him back up with Traveler."

"Fine."

As she rode away, Dylan broodingly decided that horses were much easier to figure out than women.

"What are you doing back so soon?" Raj asked Abigail as she stormed into the kitchen. "And wasn't that Dylan's horse I saw you riding in on? Did something happen?" Seeing the look on Abigail's face, she said, "Stupid question. Of course something happened. Care to talk about it?"

"I'm going to cry," Abigail warned her, reaching for a big box of facial tissue.

"That's okay. The guys have all had breakfast and are out of the way for a while." Putting her arm around Abigail's shoulders, Raj hugged her. "Tell me what happened."

"I f-fell..." Abigail choked before the tears got too much for her.

"You fell...from the horse? Are you okay? Did you break anything?"

"My h-h-heart."

"Start at the beginning," Raj suggested, guiding her over to a kitchen chair and putting a fresh cup of coffee in front of her.

Once several handfuls of tissues had been used to wipe away her tears, Abigail began, "Dylan kidnapped me yesterday."

"He did *what?* He left a note saying you two were touring the property."

"He kidnapped me."

"You mean like for a ransom or something?"

"No, I mean like the old-fashioned Gypsy tradition of kidnapping a bride."

Raj lifted one dark eyebrow. "A bride?"

"That was my reaction."

"I gather congratulations are not in order, though."

"You've got that right. He didn't mean it."

"Didn't mean what?"

"Anything. He was just kidding around."

"The lout!"

Abigail nodded. "He's a no-good, cactus-eating rat bag."

"He certainly is."

"No, he's not," Abigail wailed, the tears starting up again. "He can be sweet and funny, and his kisses are incredible.... I guess it's not his fault that he doesn't love me."

"Then he's stupid," Raj declared. "Where is he, dare I ask?"

Abigail's tears turned to a damp smile at the sound of Raj's hesitant expression. "I didn't murder him, if that's what you're wondering."

"How about leaving him stranded naked in a river?" Raj asked, referring to a scene in the new book Abigail was writing. "Did you do that?"

Abigail had had the chance to do that yesterday, but instead she'd cavorted like a wanton woman in the water with him. Well, actually she hadn't turned into a totally wanton woman until they'd gotten into bed.

But then, Dylan had hardly been an innocent bystander. His passion had matched hers; there had been no hiding how much he'd wanted her. But wanting and loving were two very different things. She'd been wanted before. She had yet to be loved.

Not that what she'd shared with Dylan last night had been like anything she'd ever experienced before, because it wasn't. She'd felt things with him, done things with him, that she'd never dreamed of. But she'd done them and felt them because she loved him. And that was the difference between her and Dylan—a difference as immense as the Grand Canyon. Love...a small, four-letter word that made Abigail cry.

Following the premise that when it rained, it poured, Abigail's father called her later that morning.

"Have you gotten it out of your system yet?" he asked her.

She certainly hadn't gotten Dylan out of her system, but her dad had no way of knowing about Abigail's broken heart. "Gotten what out of my system?"

"Running my brother's ranch."

It wasn't the first time that she noticed how her father relegated people as to how they related to *him*. No one had his or her own identity or, most often, even a name. She was always referred to as "my daughter," never "Abigail." And the phrase "my daughter" was usually followed by some comment about a harebrained idea she was entertaining.

Even getting her library degree hadn't pleased him. "Folks won't be needing librarians anymore, I read an article in the newspaper that said so. You'd have done better..." He varied the rest of the sentence from time to time, but the bottom line was that her father always thought she could have done better doing what *he* wanted her to do.

"The ranch and I are both doing fine, Dad. Thanks for asking."

Her slight edge of sarcasm went unnoticed by her father, just as she'd known it would.

"By the time you decide to sell the place, Redkins's offer could be much lower," he warned her.

"This isn't a whim, you know," Abigail told him for perhaps the twentieth time since she'd inherited the ranch from her uncle in the late spring. "I'm not going to suddenly wake up one morning and get bored with running a ranch."

"I did," her father told her.

"You didn't get bored," Abigail retorted. "You couldn't resist the money Redkins offered you."

"Family ranching is a dying proposition. Half this state is being turned into condos and ski slopes. The ranches that do survive are part of huge combines. Now, I know you've got this hankering after the past, you writing about history of the old West and all, but the time comes when you have to be realistic about things."

Realistic about things. Like the fact that Dylan didn't love her. Maybe that was why she wrote fiction. Because reality stank.

* * *

To her surprise, Ziggy dropped by just after lunch bearing a gift, which made Abigail wonder if Raj hadn't contacted him.

"How do you like it?" Ziggy asked, throwing out his chest proudly.

Uncertain what *it* was, Abigail said, "It's very nice."

"It was going to be a sculpture, then a bench, now I do not know what it is, but I thought you might like it," Ziggy said, placing the odd combination of tree branches and chunks of wood on the living-room floor, where it teetered on the old rag rug. "Perhaps it will make you smile?"

She did smile, although it wasn't the brilliant wattage that her friends were accustomed to.

"You want I should hog-tie that varmint cowboy of yours?" Ziggy asked her.

"You've been watching Raj's old Westerns again, haven't you?"

Ziggy nodded.

"Thanks for the offer, Ziggy, but—"

"You know I was married four times, yes?" Ziggy interrupted her.

"I knew you were married," she agreed. "Not that you did it four times."

"With such a history, a man learns a thing or two."

"Or three or four," Abigail couldn't resist adding.

"It is not always natural for a man to settle down. The advantages of such a thing need to be pointed out to him."

"Is that what your wives did? Point out the advantages of settling down? I'm sorry, Ziggy, but from where I'm sitting it doesn't look like they had much success at it."

Ziggy shrugged, his red-and-black-plaid flannel shirt contrasting with his yellow pants. "Ah, but the trying of it was very enjoyable while it lasted."

"It's that last part I'm not so keen on," Abigail said. "But thanks for the effort at cheering me up. I'm lucky to have such good friends as you and Raj."

"And we are lucky to have you. I know—" Ziggy clapped his hands together excitedly "—I will make fondue for you tonight, yes?"

"That would be great, thanks. It's been a long time since I've had your fondue."

"The summer, it is nearing an end now," Ziggy noted with a nod toward the window. "The nights they are getting cold."

The end of August was only a week away. Abigail had noticed the signs: the squirrels gathering up food for the winter, the cottonwood trees already sporting a few yellow leaves in amid the green. "Yeah, time is running out," she murmured.

It was useless; she couldn't get any work done. So she decided to do something that had been on her to-do list all summer—sanding and painting the crooked porch swing.

"Dylan ain't good enough for you," Randy declared.

Startled, she jerked her hand, the paintbrush dripping white paint onto the porch. "I didn't see you standing there, Randy."

"You never see me. Seems these days you've only got eyes for Dylan."

"At the moment, I've only got eyes for this swing," she retorted.

"I can do that for you. You know, you've only got to ask, and I'd do anything for you."

"I appreciate that, Randy, but..." Something about his hot gaze was making her feel uncomfortable.

"You deserve the best of everything. Dylan can't give you that. He's too young for you."

Abigail didn't appreciate that observation. "Yes, well..."

"I've read your books, you know. I know whole passages by heart. Go on, ask me to recite a part. Any part."

"That's okay. I believe you."

"No, go on, ask me."

"Really, it's not necessary."

Randy went ahead and recited the opening to her last two books, word for word.

"My father doesn't know it, but I've got a great memory," Randy bragged.

"I can see you do." Abigail was feeling *real* uncomfortable now. "Weren't you supposed to be cleaning the horse stalls this afternoon?"

"I finished that work already. This is more important."

"What is?"

"Talking to you..."

"I'm flattered, but there really is plenty of work to be done on the ranch...."

"You won't have to worry about that. I've taken care of things for you."

That had a somewhat ominous ring to it. "What do you mean?" she asked.

"I mean that I've taken care of things for you," Randy repeated. "A beautiful woman like you shouldn't have to worry about the details of running a ranch like this. It will make you old before your time."

Another quote from one of her books, she thought to herself, wishing Raj would come outside before remembering her friend had gone into Big Rock to pick up groceries and a new batch of Western videos she'd ordered by mail.

"You really don't have to worry about me," Abigail tried reassuring Randy.

"I know I don't. Because I've taken care of things. I'd like to show you want I mean."

"Another time, maybe. As you can see, I'm right in the middle of repainting this old swing."

"I'll wait."

"No, I wouldn't want you to do that."

"Then I'll paint it for you."

"No!" When he tried to take the paintbrush from her, she held on to it for all she was worth. "Really, I'd rather do it myself."

To her relief, Randy backed off. "Okay, if that's what you want."

"It is."

"Guess I'll ride on up to help my dad and Dylan with those fences."

"Good idea," Abigail said.

After he'd gone, she told herself she was just getting oversensitive. Randy hadn't said anything wrong, although reciting memorized passages of her books was a little weird. She shook her head. She was making too much of things. It must just be that her feelings were confused by Dylan.

Just as she'd put the last coat of paint on the swing about an hour later, Randy came galloping in, yelling, "Dylan's hurt. There was an accident. He's asking for you, Abbie. I think you better hurry."

"Why can't women just come right out and say what they mean? I don't think it's too much to ask, do you? I mean, look at how well you and I get along. We don't have any trouble communicating. You always know what I'm talking about, you can sense my moods, you know my routine, we're comfortable together. Why is it that you're the only one who understands me?'' Dylan asked Traveler while undoing the saddle cinch. ''And why am I standing here talking to my horse? Not that I don't enjoy our talks, you know I do. Remember the good old days, when we'd ride in the opening parades? I swear you got as many cheers as I did, being the fine specimen that you are.''

Traveler snorted and blew air through his flared nostrils in equine agreement.

To reward him, Dylan added more oats to Traveler's feed before heading on over to the ranch house. He knew he wouldn't be getting a warm welcome from Abbie.

He still wasn't sure where things had gone wrong this morning. One second, they'd been snuggled together in bed, and the next minute, she'd taken off in a huff. He knew it had something to do with his reaction to her saying the word *wedding*.

But she'd said she'd only been kidding and then added the kicker, that he wasn't the kind of man she was looking for. What the hell was that supposed to mean? How was a man supposed to know if she was mad at him for bringing up marriage or for trying to duck out of it?

As he neared the front porch, Dylan saw the orange barn cat sitting on the railing near the swing. He remembered how that cat had stuck her nose in the air after the fight Dylan had had with Abigail in the barn last week. Ever since then, the cat had been distant with him. Just like Abbie. Until last night. Abbie hadn't been distant last night. She'd been . . . incredible.

Deciding to practice his "making up" skills, Dylan approached the cat. "So, are you not speaking to me, either, hmm? I didn't mean anything insulting before, but you've got to admit that males do have a hard time figuring out the female of the species, whatever the species."

"Abbie just painted that swing this afternoon so I wouldn't get too close to it if I were you. It's probably still wet," Raj warned him as she stood in the doorway, a kitchen towel in her hands.

"I can see that. Where is Abbie, by the way?"

"I don't know. She wasn't here when I got back from Big Rock. She must have left in a hurry—the can of paint and the brush were still out here on the porch. Her horse is gone. So is Randy's."

This news immediately raised an internal red flag as far as Dylan was concerned. "It'll be time for supper soon."

"I know. She should have been back by now. I'm getting worried about her. When I left, she didn't say anything about going riding. In fact, she was expecting an important call from her agent."

"Maybe the agent called, and Abbie decided to go for a ride."

"That's the thing. The phone was ringing when I got in, and it was Abbie's agent. She still hadn't reached Abbie. And this was a *very* important call. Abbie wouldn't have blown it off like this unless something happened."

"Well, she was sort of upset...." Dylan began.

"Because of you." Raj's look was a piercing accusation.

Not knowing how much Abbie had told her friend about what had gone on at the homesteader's cabin last night, Dylan was at a temporary loss as to what to say.

The telltale sound of the musical horn on Ziggy's four-wheel-drive vehicle diverted Dylan's attention.

Ziggy approached Dylan with a thunderous expression. "Abbie iz too goot vur you," he growled, his accent even more noticeable than normal.

"Have you seen her?" Dylan demanded.

"Of course. I am here to make fondue for her."

"She isn't here," Raj told Ziggy.

"But I told her I was coming at this time. Where is she? I talked to her this afternoon, and she said she would be here. She was going to paint the swing."

"When was the last time you saw Abbie?" Dylan asked Ziggy.

"This afternoon. Maybe three o'clock. Randy and Abbie went by riding hell-bent for leather a few hours ago."

"And you didn't find any note or anything in the house when you got home?" Dylan asked Raj.

She shook her head. "Do you think something happened to them?"

"It's unlikely. Look, there's Shem and Hondo coming back, maybe they know what's going on."

"Shem might, but Hondo never has known what's going on in the past, so I seriously doubt if he will know anything now," Raj muttered.

"Shem, have you seen Abbie or Randy?" Dylan asked.

The older man shook his head. "No, can't say that I have."

"Did Randy say anything about going riding with Abbie today?"

"Randy hasn't been saying much of anything to me lately," Shem admitted. "He's been acting mighty peculiar, even for him."

"What do you mean?"

"Well, I don't mean to be impugning my son's reputation none, but he's been gone a lot, not been keeping up with all his chores."

"Where does he go?"

"That's just it. He won't say. I interrogated him about the matter, but he remained recalcitrant."

"Don't they have medicine for that?" Hondo asked.

"I don't like this," Dylan muttered. "I don't like the sound of this one bit."

"Where are you going?" Shem asked him.

"To see if I can find Abbie."

"Randy would never hurt her."

"He better not, or he's dead meat." Dylan's voice was as rock hard as the surrounding Bitterroot Mountains.

"He's sweet on her," Hondo blurted out. "Made me promise not to tell."

"Great," Dylan muttered.

"And he's not real happy with you," Hondo continued.

"Well, the feeling is mutual," Dylan growled. "Come on, the four of us will ride out, fanning out in each direction. Ziggy, you use your Jeep and go south. Hondo, you go east, and Shem, you take the ground to the west. I'll go north."

"What about me?" Raj asked.

"You stay here in case she should come back to the ranch house."

"Classic Western," Raj muttered as the men departed. "Leave the little woman behind to mind the fire." In a louder voice, she called out, "Dylan, take Abbie's cellular phone with you. She's got it recharging in the barn. Call in and bring her home."

Dylan's first stop was the hill behind the ranch house, the one he'd kidnapped her from...was it just yesterday? But there was no sign of her today. He called out her name, afraid that she might have taken cover when she'd heard him coming. Not that she'd be in the best mood to answer him, either.

"Ziggy is here for fondue. Come on, Abbie, if you're up here, let me know. I won't bother you, I promise. I just need to know you're okay."

But his words were only answered by the wind and a noisy magpie. Golden sunlight hit the hilltop, reminding Dylan of how the sunlight hit Abbie's blond hair, turning it into spun gold. The smell of wood smoke from the ranch-house fireplace reminded him of the fireplace at the homesteader's cabin, and Abbie's teasing comment about him knowing how to start fires and his comment about not being able to control them. The same might be said about relationships. Dylan knew how to get things started, but keeping the fire going, tending to it and making sure the embers didn't burn out—that wasn't anything he had any experience with.

His own parents had been married forever, it seemed. It was a happy marriage. But since Dylan had started chasing rodeo, he'd seen few happy marriages. The life-style didn't leave much time for family and all too much opportunity for trouble. But Dylan didn't have that life anymore. He didn't know what life he did have, but in that instant it hit him that he wanted Abbie in his life.

He might be a rolling stone, but he'd never lost anything he'd ever really missed. Until now. Until Abbie.

His stomach clenched, and his hand sought the reassurance of the red button in his shirt pocket. It had come off Abigail's shirt before they'd made love last night. He'd found it after she'd gone galloping off and left him alone. As a kid, his dad had always told him that finding something red, like a button, was a sign of good luck.

Dylan sure hoped so. Because he was getting a very bad feeling.

It was the same kind of feeling in the pit of his stomach he used to get in the chutes, a sixth sense that would warn him something was about to go wrong. He'd ignored that feeling at his own expense that last go-round, and he'd bit the dust big time, smashing his leg when a horse named Devil Dare had gotten the better of him.

Dylan had that same concrete-butterfly-in-the-gut feeling again now. And this time, he wasn't about to ignore his instincts. This time, he wasn't going to take any risks. He was going to find Abbie.

Nine

The sun had set and the twilight shadows darkened to blackness when Dylan returned to the ranch house. He knew even before Raj told him that Abbie still hadn't been found.

"Nothing?" Dylan asked, his voice ragged.

Raj shook her head.

"I learned tracking in army," Ziggy said. "I found some tracks where I saw Randy and Abbie riding, but they went into the river."

"Randy is trying to cover his tracks," Raj said. "They do that in the movies all the time."

"I'm calling the police," Dylan said.

"I already did that," Raj replied. "The sheriff said he'd be here an hour ago. Ah, maybe that's him now."

Sure enough, Sheriff Tiber came driving up, as if he had all the time in the world. Already Dylan was ready to throttle him.

"Misplaced your boss, have ya?" Sheriff Tiber laughed before spitting a wad of tobacco out of the side of his mouth.

It was all Dylan could do not to grab the weasely lawman by the throat and slam him against his fancy police car. But that would only land Dylan in jail, and he couldn't do Abigail any good there. So he kept his cool.

"She's been missing since early this afternoon," he said curtly.

"Well like I tol' your little foreign friend over there on the phone, I can't call out a search party until daylight. You say she rode off with Randy Buskirk? Maybe the two of them are sparkin' and snugglin' under the stars somewheres."

"And maybe Hoss Redkins took her to do a little personal convincing that she should sell this ranch," Dylan shot back.

"You watch your mouth, boy. I haven't forgot about you pullin' somethin' fishy at the dance, resultin' in Hoss Jr. injurin' himself. Charges might still be pressed against you regardin' that incident."

Not the least bit intimidated by the threat, Dylan retorted, "Last I heard, it wasn't illegal to look at someone."

"It might be in this county," Shem muttered.

"What did you say, old man?" Sheriff Tiber demanded.

"I said that it might be that in this county, folks don't have the percipience to know what they've got with you as their lawman," Shem said.

Sheriff Tiber frowned, clearly unsure if he'd just been complimented or insulted.

"I hardly ever know what he's talkin' about, either," Hondo told the sheriff in sympathy.

"If Abigail is still missing by tomorrow, I'll see if I can get a man to come out and help in the search," the sheriff said. "But she's got to be missing twenty-four hours before I can do that."

Shem's hand on Dylan's arm prevented him from doing something he might regret. Dylan froze, remembering how Abbie had always been the one to put her hand on his arm. Would he ever see her again?

In the past, the thing Dylan had always feared the most in life was losing his freedom. But now, with Abbie's disappearance, he realized that the thing he *really* feared the most was losing her.

Dylan watched the red taillights of the sheriff's car until they disappeared in the darkness. It had been a while since Dylan had prayed, but he prayed now, prayed that Abbie wasn't hurt, that she was okay, that he'd find her.

Then he went inside and phoned Hoss Redkins.

"He's out of town on business," a Mexican woman told him.

"Tell him that I'm holding him personally responsible for Abbie Turner's safety," Dylan grated before slamming down the phone.

"Maybe I should just drive over there myself," he muttered. "Maybe he's got her at the ranch."

"His wife would never go along with that," Shem stated.

"There are plenty of places on his spread to hide out."

"We don't know Redkins is behind her disappearance. She rode out with Randy," Shem reminded him.

So Dylan's options were that either she'd been kidnapped by a lovestruck cowboy or she'd been taken by an overbearing bully who wanted her land. Neither scenario boded real well as far as Dylan was concerned. He was seriously considering driving over to Redkins's place himself when the phone rang.

"It's for you," Raj told him.

Thinking it might be news about Abigail, Dylan grabbed the phone. "Hello?"

"Hey, little brother, how are things going in the damsel-rescuing business?" Michael cheerfully inquired.

"She's gone."

"Who? What's going on up there?"

"Abbie. She went out riding with one of the hands this afternoon, and neither one of them has come back. The local sheriff won't do diddly squat. I've got this gut feeling that she's in trouble, maybe hurt. I've got to find her. Listen, I can't talk now. I've got to go." Dylan hung up the phone.

Not even five seconds later, it rang again. He automatically picked it up.

"Put Dylan Janos on the phone," a muffled voice demanded.

"This is Dylan."

"If you ever want to see your girlfriend Abbie alive, you'll ride out to the high-country cabin—alone. At dawn. You get there any earlier or later, and she's a goner."

"You hurt one hair on her head..." Dylan growled, but he was speaking to silence. The caller, whoever it was, had already hung up.

"Randy, you know what's going to happen," Abbie said, using what the librarians at work would have recognized as her analytical voice. It was the one she used on the library director whenever he wanted to cut the budget. Now she wanted to cut the rope Randy had used to hobble her to the cabin's center support beam. "They're going to come looking for me."

"Not in the dark. And even if they do, they won't know to look for you here. Not until we want him to."

"Him, who? Who are you talking about?"

"Dylan. Who else?"

"What do you have against Dylan? What do you have against me? Why are you doing this?"

"You should never have come up here to this cabin with Dylan."

"Why not?"

"I can't talk about it. You sure you don't want something to eat?"

Abigail shook her head, trying to keep her fingers from shaking. Randy had tied her right ankle and wrist to the cabin's center support beam together, effectively hobbling her. Then he sat about two feet away from her, never taking his eyes off her so she could test the intricate knots he'd tied. He'd moved the bed closer to the center post so she could sit on it.

Abigail had ridden all the way out here thinking that Dylan had been hurt, that he was lying up here injured. It hadn't been until she'd rushed into the cabin that she'd realized something was wrong. The place had been deserted, the wildflowers she'd picked when Dylan had kidnapped her as his make-believe bride already dried up in the mason jar.

The bed where she and Dylan had made love offered her no comfort now. Instead, it was a mocking reminder of everything that had gone wrong. She still couldn't believe everything that had happened in the past thirty-six hours. She'd been kidnapped, wooed, skinny-dipped, smoked out, courted, kissed, caressed and made love to.

After that, things had gone downhill fast, starting with her humiliation about misunderstanding Dylan's intentions. Her heart had been broken, and she'd been furious, hurt, depressed. Then Randy had told her Dylan had been hurt, and she'd been panic-stricken, anxious, kidnapped again. Only this time, she was *not* having a good time. In fact, she was scared, even though she was trying not to show it.

"Randy, can't you loosen this rope?"

"I'd really like to, but I can't risk you taking off."

"And what's going to happen when I have to visit the outhouse?"

"I'll go with you and stand guard outside."

"Great," she muttered.

"This wasn't all my idea," Randy said defensively.

"Then whose idea was it?"

"I can't tell you that."

Five minutes later, Abigail asked, "Are you going to start a fire? It's getting chilly in here."

"Good idea."

Abigail had it all mapped out. The blocked chimney would fill the cabin with smoke. Randy would have to untie her and take her outside. In the confusion, she'd make her getaway. It was a great plan.

Unfortunately the chimney did not cooperate.

"Ah, that's a nice fire going now. Some birds had put a nest in the chimney flue, but I cleared that out right after Dylan left this morning."

"You mean you were up here spying on us?" The thought of Randy seeing her as she'd gone skinny-dipping, or when she'd made love with Dylan in the candlelit cabin, made her skin crawl.

"I only got here in time to see you go riding off alone on that big Appaloosa of his. But I knew what you'd been up to up here. And I won't hold it against you. I know that none of that was your idea.''

''None of this is my idea, either. I'd much rather be back home.''

''I know that. I'm trying to make it as comfortable up here as possible. Now, I'm not a man to go getting my feelings hurt easily, but I think you could be a bit more understanding about how difficult this is on me.''

''Difficult on *you?*'' she repeated in disbelief. ''You should try it from where I'm sitting.''

''How about I read you some excerpts from your last book? I think I resemble Ramon, don't you?''

The way a chipmunk resembled a lion. Instead of answering, she said, ''Don't read my book.'' She knew from the look on his face that he'd planned on reading her the love scenes. She didn't want him getting any ideas. ''Tell me about yourself instead.'' She could only hope to keep him busy until help came.

''Who was on the phone?'' Raj asked.

''My brother, Michael, from Chicago.''

''Both times?''

Dylan didn't know whom to trust. Raj had been Abbie's friend for years. But how was he to know if she was involved in this mess? He just couldn't risk it. Not with Abbie's well-being at risk.

Dylan decided he'd do better doing this alone. He worked best that way. Traveled faster, too.

But he didn't want to be alone anymore. He wanted to be with Abbie.

''That was your brother calling both times?'' Raj repeated.

''Yeah, I hung up on him so fast the first time he forgot to tell me something important.''

"Oh. I was hoping it might be news of Abbie."

"Yeah, me too."

As Dylan approached the homesteader's cabin at dawn the next morning, he marveled at what a difference a day made. Yesterday at about this time, he and Abigail had been in that cabin, snuggling together in bed. Now he didn't even know if she was dead or alive.

He'd told himself all night that it was in her kidnapper's best interest to keep her alive. And he'd dreamed up and discarded at least half a dozen bold rescue attempts. But none of them could guarantee her safety. He could only hope that him showing up here would do that.

He'd barely dismounted from his horse when Randy showed up out of nowhere with a hunting rifle. "Hands on your head," he ordered.

Dylan obeyed. He didn't have much choice. "Where's Abbie? She better not be hurt, or the buzzards are gonna pick your bones, Randy."

"I would never hurt Abbie. You're the one who did that," Randy retorted.

Dylan winced, because he knew that Randy was right. He *had* hurt Abbie. But that was a mistake he'd never make again.

"Is your boss here?" Dylan demanded.

Randy nodded. "Inside."

"And Abbie?"

"She's in there, too. Go on, get a move on." Randy shoved Dylan up the step to the front door.

The cabin was dimly lit with the weak morning sunlight just starting to filter through the windows. Dylan's first concern was Abbie. He found her sitting on the bed.

"Abbie, are you okay?" He immediately moved toward her, but was stopped by the end of a rifle. This one was held by none other than Hoss Jr.

"I'm fine," Abigail hastily assured Dylan.

"Hi there, Junior. Your daddy send you to do his dirty work?" Dylan drawled.

"This has nothing to do with my daddy," Hoss Jr. stated. "He doesn't know anything about this because he thinks small. My plans are more global in nature."

"And what plans might that be?"

"Importing a big cash crop over the Canadian border," Hoss Jr. replied. "The border runs along the northeastern property line of this ranch, you know. Old Pete never paid any attention to what was going on up here, he was too old to get around much anyway. But I knew that wouldn't last once the new owner took over. That's why I pushed for my dad to buy this place."

"*You're* the one who wanted Redkins to buy this ranch?"

Hoss Jr. nodded. "You see, I couldn't let anything jeopardize the nice little operation I've set up here."

"What kind of cash crop are you talking about?" Abigail demanded. "Are you rustling cattle or something?"

Hoss Jr. just laughed. "This is something much more lucrative."

"Drugs," Dylan said.

"Nothing really bad," Randy inserted. "Just marijuana."

"And how did *you* get wrapped up in this mess?"

"I needed the money," Randy said.

"Why drag Abbie and me into this?"

"That's all your fault," Randy accused. "If you'd just have minded your own business and kept on riding, none of this would have happened. I was supposed to be the one to rescue Abbie that first day in the meadow, not you. I had it all planned out."

"So you're the one who put the burrs under that saddle blanket?" Dylan asked.

Randy nodded. "Wild Thing may not like strangers much, but I'd been taking care of her for a month so she trusted me."

Dylan growled, "Why, you son of a . . ."

In the blink of an eye, Dylan had Randy by the shirt collar and was shaking him the way a terrier shakes a rat, when Hoss Jr. suddenly kicked Dylan's bad leg out from under him.

Dylan managed to save himself from falling flat on his face, but he had to let go of Randy to do so.

"Gee, Junior, it looks like your toe wasn't broken that night of the dance after all," Dylan drawled, gritting his teeth against the pain shooting down his right leg.

"No thanks to you," Hoss Jr. retorted. "My father isn't the brightest man in the state. It wasn't very courteous of you to play on his lack of intelligence with all those ridiculous threats about some Gypsy curse."

"I take that to mean that giving you the evil eye won't work?" Dylan inquired.

"Bingo."

"Then I'll just have to come up with something else, won't I?"

"I'll give you this, Janos. You don't give up easily. I admire your spirit. Under other circumstances, we might have worked together."

"Not in this lifetime."

"Well, maybe in your next lifetime, then. Because your time is running out on this one."

"Abbie was supposed to lean on me," Randy declared. "I would have been her rescuer, not you. And when I slashed her tires, she was supposed to come to me. She was supposed to fall in love with *me*. Not you."

"Look," Dylan said placatingly, "why don't you let Abbie go...?"

"How chivalrous of you," Hoss Jr. inserted. "But that won't work. Abbie has to be gotten rid of. That way, the ranch will revert to her father, who has already said he thinks the ranch should be sold to my father. Once that happens, dear old Dad will never think to check the northeastern corner of this holding. Why should he? He's got his only son looking after things for him."

"His only son, the drug runner."

"Marijuana is just another crop as far as I'm concerned."

"How noble of you."

"We tried things Randy's way. I gave him the chance to scare her into selling. But she got stubborn."

"Yeah, that's a trait she's got," Dylan had to admit, all the while trying to come up with a way out of this mess.

"But you said you weren't going to hurt Abbie," Randy belatedly protested, only now registering what Hoss Jr. had said. "I'm not going to stand here and let you hurt Abbie."

"Then you'll have to *sit*...over there!" Hoss Jr. pointed his gun at Randy and then at the bed. "Tie him up, Janos."

"Why should I?" Dylan knew that Hoss Jr. had no intention of letting them go. It didn't take a brain surgeon to figure out that they knew too much. The way Dylan saw it, having Randy as a distraction was in their best interest. Now, if he could just get Randy to help out...

"Because I'll shoot Abbie if you don't. Oh, never mind," Hoss Jr. muttered in disgust. "If you want anything done right, you've got to do it yourself." Without further ado, he clubbed Randy with the rifle, knocking him unconscious. "There, one less idiot to worry about."

"Are you this good to all your employees?" Dylan mockingly inquired.

"You think you're so smart? Working for a dumb romance writer?" Hoss laughed cruelly.

"I am not dumb," Abigail declared with dignity before realizing dignity was lost on a rattlesnake like Hoss Jr. So she let her anger take hold, shouting, *I am not dumb!*

"Yeah, right," Hoss Jr. mocked. "Like yelling at a man holding a gun on you and your bucking cowboy lover isn't dumb? Right." His laughter increased.

"I *don't* like being laughed at," Abigail growled, putting her hands on the table and leaning forward to make her point.

The table, never steady under the best of circumstances, turned over with a loud crash.

It was just the opening Dylan needed. He made his move....

Ten

Dylan managed to knock the rifle from Hoss Jr.'s hands. The gun landed on the cabin floor, but before Dylan could reach for it, Hoss Jr. had landed a punch right in Dylan's abdomen.

Abigail winced on his behalf even as she struggled against the ropes holding her captive. But no matter how she squirmed, the rifle remained just out of her reach.

Even as she attempted to get her hands on the gun, she was very much aware of the fight going on around her. Dylan was faster than Hoss Jr., but Hoss Jr. weighed about three times as much. His fists were the size of hams, and he was pounding them on Dylan, who was managing to hold his own despite the odds. When Dylan landed a swift left hook smack on Hoss Jr.'s jaw, Abigail jumped up and down and screamed, "Get him! Get him!"

Unfortunately her words distracted Dylan, allowing Hoss Jr. to punch him . . . hard.

Frantic, Abigail strained against the ropes and tried even harder to reach the rifle. Just a little more . . . just another inch . . .

She had her fingertips on the barrel of the rifle when the fighting men stumbled backward, nearly smashing her fingers and sending the rifle skidding against the far wall. There was no way she could reach it now! Her right ankle and wrist were still tied to the upright support beam in the center of the cabin, hobbling her and giving her *very* limited mobility.

"Oh, fudge," she wailed.

Hoss Jr. paused to snicker at her choice of curses before turning his back on her and hitting Dylan again.

Infuriated, Abigail used her free left hand to grab the heavy mason jar, which had somehow miraculously avoided breaking when the table had tipped over. Holding the jar high over her head, she waited for the right moment as the two men struggled. Dylan, Hoss Jr., Dylan, Hoss Jr.—their heads whirled by like a kid's top.

Duck and dodge . . . okay, here he came. . . .

Smash!

She'd brought the heavy glass jar down with all her might, crashing it on Hoss Jr.'s head. As the big man slid to the cabin floor, Abigail dusted her hand on her thigh and reminded the prone figure, "I told you I didn't like being laughed at."

"My hero!" Dylan murmured with a lift of one devilish eyebrow.

"Oh, Dylan!" She threw her one free arm around him, tugging him closer so that both arms reached around him.

Dylan returned her embrace. "Let me untie you first," he said, brushing her lips with a kiss that was filled with promise and something else. . . .

The moment she was free, Dylan lifted her right arm to kiss the inside of her wrist, where the skin was raw and red from her struggles to get free. "You poor baby," he crooned against her skin.

Hoss Jr. groaned at their feet, reminding them of his presence. With amazing speed and efficiency, Dylan used the rope that had been used on Abigail to tie up Hoss Jr.—tying him the way he'd tie a calf at a calf-roping event—arms and legs tied together in one neat package.

"Give that cowboy a 99," Abigail cheered, as if judging the event.

Dylan looked up and flashed her that special grin of his. His black Stetson had been knocked off early in the fight. Standing up, he held his arms out to her, and she rushed into them.

"I was so afraid he'd hurt you. Oh, your poor lip." Her tender touch was as light as thistledown as she brushed her fingertip across the perfection of his mouth, now marred slightly by a split lip.

"It's nothing," he dismissed before growling, "I was afraid *you* were hurt." His desperado voice was gruff and dusty. "Are you sure you're okay? They didn't hurt you? I couldn't bear it if anything happened to you."

"Oh, Dylan. . ." She pressed a string of loving kisses along the uninjured corner of his mouth.

Being the creative type, Dylan kept the pressure of his mouth resting on hers light and instead intensified the kiss with the use of his tongue, which, after all, hadn't been injured in the fight.

The thrust and parry, the sweeping dalliance, made Abigail go weak at the knees. It also made her want more.

She was pressed against him as tightly as paper stuck to a window in a gale-force wind. It didn't seem to be close enough for Dylan, who stroked her from her nape to the small of her back, fitting her against him and rubbing against her with hungry need.

Feeling him wince as she ran her fingertips across his jaw, she broke off the kiss. "You were so brave, coming up here by yourself to save me...."

Dylan just shrugged. "You know what they say—when all else fails, be brave. We have a phrase for it in rodeo. You might have heard it. Cowboy up."

"It certainly is," she noted with a grin, moving against his obvious arousal.

He gave her a supposedly reprimanding frown even as he held her tighter. "I'm trying to be serious here."

"*That* will be the day."

"Today *is* the day. The day that I ask you to marry me."

Putting her hands on his chest, she shoved him away and gave him a reproachful glare. "That's not funny."

"I wasn't trying to be funny. This is just as tough on me as it is on you...."

"Gosh, what a romantic proposal," she noted wryly with a shake of her head. "Telling me that marrying me would be tough..."

"I meant the *asking*."

"I haven't heard any asking yet."

"Will you marry me?"

"Why should I?" she countered.

"Because I love you, you infuriating woman. My wandering days are over." Smoothing her wavy hair from her forehead, he quietly said, "I've found my freedom in you. Now, are you going to marry me or not?"

Given what they'd just been through, the fact that Dylan was younger than she was didn't seem very relevant anymore. The fact that he was alive and loved her was the important thing. "Yes," she whispered. "Yes, I'll marry you."

With a loud "Ya-hooo!" Dylan swooped down to capture her mouth with his, momentarily forgetting his split lip as he gathered her against him.

In the safe haven of his arms, Abigail knew with bone-deep certainty that this was where she was meant to be. Just as the mountains had provided her with an inherent sense of peace, so too did Dylan's embrace give her a strong sense of joy.

At first, the strange *whap-whap-whap* sound seemed to be the blood thrumming through her head. Then it finally occurred to her that the noise was coming from above her head—and above Dylan's, too, for that matter.

Reluctantly lifting his parted lips from hers, Dylan muttered, "Damn, I almost forgot...."

"Forgot what? What is that noise?"

"A helicopter." Opening the front door, Dylan went outside, but instead of trying to wave to get the helicopter's attention, he reached into his saddlebags and tugged out her cellular phone.

"I knew Sheriff Tiber wouldn't do anything, so I called in reinforcements from outside his jurisdiction." Into the phone, he said, "Dylan here. We're ready for you now." After he'd flipped shut the phone, he saw the look Abigail was giving him. "What?"

"Correct me if I'm wrong, but weren't you the man who made this awful face—" she did a passable impression "—when I talked about using a cellular phone?"

"When?"

"That first day when you rescued me. I told you I'd gotten a call from my editor on my cellular phone, and you made this face—" she screwed up her face like a kid facing a plateful of spinach "—as if I were some kind of Hollywood type or something."

"I remember thinking you must be very high maintenance."

"And what do you think now?"

"That I can't live without you," he said simply.

He would have taken her in his arms, but since the chopper swooped out of the sky, he had to make do with putting an arm around her shoulder as he calmed Traveler and Wild Thing.

The helicopter landed in a nearby clearing, close enough to make fast work of picking up Hoss Jr. and Randy but far enough away not to freak out the horses.

The arrival of the police made everything seem so much more tangible. She shivered and burrowed closer to Dylan.

"We'll drive in to Missoula later and give a statement," Dylan told the officials.

Abigail didn't relax until the helicopter had disappeared over the mountaintops.

"You know what I'd like to do now?"

"Does it have anything to do with strawberries and whipped cream?" he asked with a wicked lift of one devil-dark eyebrow.

She smiled. "It might. I really want to go home, take a long, hot shower and . . ."

"And?"

"And make love with you."

"Sounds like a plan," he declared.

She tugged her paint-stained work shirt from her body as she said, "It's just that I've been in the same clothes since yesterday. I almost made my escape last night, you know. I'd come up with this brilliant plan, asking Randy to build a fire, knowing that the chimney was plugged. I figured that he'd have to untie me to get me outside of the cabin and then I'd run for it…but he'd cleared the bird's nest out."

"I wonder if it was a robin's nest," Dylan murmured. "My dad always said it's bad luck to mess with a robin's nest. Guess Randy just proved him right."

Because Dylan didn't want to let Abbie go for even one second, he had her ride with him on Traveler while Wild Thing trailed behind.

"This brings back memories," she murmured, leaning back against his chest. "What is this now, the third time I've been in your saddle?"

"My saddle is ready for you now," he growled, his voice silky and sexy as he spoke into her ear. He slid his left hand to the inside of her thigh and crept up the double seam of her jeans until he erotically cupped her in the palm of his hand.

"You keep that up, and we're going to be riding more than just a horse, cowboy," she gasped.

She was actually considering the possibility of turning around to face him, wrapping her legs around his waist and making love on the back of his horse, when she realized they were almost home.

"I hope you plan on joining me for a hot shower," she told Dylan with a sultry smile over her shoulder. "I'll make it worth your while."

Out of the corner of her eye, she saw a group of people standing outside the ranch house. They were still too far away for her make out who they were.

"Looks like someone has sent out a search party for us."

"You could say that."

Something about the way he said that made her ask, "Who are those people?"

"My family," Dylan ruefully replied.

"Your family?" She gave him a horrified look and sat up board straight, immediately putting a more respectable distance between them. "What are they doing here? I'm not ready to meet your family," she wailed. "I look like a wreck! Like an old hag! They'll think I'm robbing the cradle."

"They'll think I'm the luckiest man on the face of the earth."

"I suppose it would be too obvious to turn the horse around and head for the hills, huh?" she inquired.

"Just relax. After what you've been through today, meeting my family will be a piece of cake."

"Yeah, right," she muttered as he pulled Traveler to a halt outside the barn.

Abigail allowed herself the indulgence of letting Dylan help her down. "How's your leg doing?" she asked in concern.

"It could use a long hot shower with a leggy blonde," he replied with a wolfish grin.

"I know just the woman for you," Abigail stated before tilting his black Stetson back and kissing him.

"Hey, baby brother, we came to help you, but I can see you have everything out here under control after all," Michael noted dryly.

"You've got that right," Dylan murmured, keeping his eyes on Abigail.

As Shem and Hondo took care of the horses, Dylan turned Abigail to introduce her to his family.

But before he could do that, Raj breathlessly burst onto the scene, and she and Abigail engaged in a huge hug-fest.

"Sorry," Raj said to Michael. "I didn't mean to intrude on a family get-together."

"You're like family. That goes for you, too, Ziggy," Abigail added as the eccentric artist came closer for a hug of his own.

While this was going on, Dylan was asking Michael, "How did you get out here so fast?"

Before Michael could answer, a whirlwind with shoulder-length dark hair threw herself into Dylan's arms. Abigail didn't know whether to be upset or not, until she saw the young woman's face. The family resemblance was clear.

"I could break every bone in your body for putting us through all this worry," Gaylynn yelled at Dylan even as she hugged him again.

Seeing the look Dylan directed at him over their sister's head, Michael shrugged and laconically explained, "Gaylynn and Hunter had come up to visit the folks in Chicago. That's why I called you last night. But when I heard about the trouble out here, Hunter and I decided we'd fly out and see if we couldn't lend a hand in getting you your lady back."

"Hunter is a police officer," Dylan said for Abigail's benefit. "And he's also been foolish enough to saddle himself with this wild sister of mine."

"Hunter has a cousin who works for the airlines—"

"Hunter has tons of cousins," Gaylynn inserted, finally releasing Dylan from her sisterly embrace.

"Anyway, he and I were going to fly out alone—"

"But Gaylynn and I wouldn't hear of it," Brett said. "Hi, I'm Brett Janos. The only normal one in this family." She held out her hand to Abigail. "I'm Michael's wife. You've probably gathered that Gaylynn there is Michael and Dylan's sister. And this quiet man standing behind me trying not to laugh is Hunter Davis, Gaylynn's husband."

"Brett isn't the only normal one in the family," Hunter said with a Southern drawl. "I'm normal, too."

"I don't know about that," Michael protested. "I heard all about your argument with a chain saw, Hunter. How normal is that?"

"That's not funny! He was almost killed," Gaylynn said, socking Michael's arm.

"Michael and Hunter have been friends since they were kids," Dylan explained to Abigail. To Michael, he said, "Where's Hope? My adorable little niece should be able to say her Uncle Dylan's name by now."

"The folks are watching her back in Chicago," Michael said. "So are you going to introduce us to the lady or not, baby brother? Nice shiner you're going to have tomorrow, by the way."

"I'm so glad you approve," Dylan drawled. "This is Abbie Turner, the woman I'm going to marry."

Abigail couldn't believe Dylan had introduced her like that, without any lead-in.

Her surprise must have shown in her eyes because Brett reached out to pat her arm consolingly. "Don't worry about it, Michael introduced me to his family just about the same way. They don't have much tact, these Janoses."

"Welcome to the family," Gaylynn said, giving Abigail a big hug. To Dylan, she said, "See, I told you that the Rom box would work its magic on you."

"What Rom box?" Abigail asked.

"You mean he didn't tell you?"

"I've been kind of busy lately," Dylan growled.

"Rescuing ladies in distress?" Michael asked.

Bemused by it all, Abigail just stood there watching them. There was obviously a lot of love between Dylan and his family. They were a loud group. The quietest one seemed to be his older brother, Michael, who had striking, light hazel eyes and a lean face with high cheekbones. Despite his joking with Dylan, there was a definite intensity about him.

In contrast, Michael's wife, Brett, was lively and outgoing. Her short dark hair and blue eyes gave her a pixie air. But the heavy-duty hiking boots and jean vest adorned with a button that said Take Time For Kids indicated that this was a practical woman with her feet on the ground.

Gaylynn was a real powerhouse with brown, blunt-cut hair and brown eyes that didn't miss a thing. She was obviously the apple of husband Hunter's eye, who was much taller than his petite wife. Hunter had a touch of silver in his brown hair and the most vivid green eyes Abigail had ever seen.

Both Hunter and Michael exuded confidence, but no more so than Dylan.

A hand on her arm drew her attention. Shem was standing beside her, awkwardly shifting from one foot to the other with a shamefaced expression on his wrinkled face. "I feel it my paternal duty to apologize for Randy's behavior," he declared. "Dylan had the authorities call me and tell me what had happened. I'm so sorry...I'll pack my things and be out of your hair tonight."

Abigail stopped his words with a hug. "It wasn't your fault, Shem. And I'd be lost if you left."

"Are you sure?"

"Positive. And don't blame yourself for what happened with Randy. If it makes you feel any better, I honestly don't think he meant to hurt me. In fact, he stood up for me to Hoss Jr."

"Thanks for telling me that," Shem murmured before nodding his farewell and taking his leave.

As he did so, it suddenly occurred to Abigail that she was still wearing the travel-worn clothes she'd had on yesterday. This family reunion would have to continue without her until after she took a shower...alone, darn it.

Ten minutes later, she was downstairs, her wet hair wrapped in a towel, wearing fresh jeans and a denim shirt and smelling of lily of the valley. It was all Dylan could do not to take her in his arms right there and then. She'd hardly been out of his sight.

Dylan fussed over her like a mother hen, setting her on the couch and putting cushions behind her back. From the incredulous and humorous looks of his sister and brother, Abigail gathered that this was a new side of Dylan.

"I'm fine," Abigail said, tugging Dylan down to sit beside her rather than having him hovering over her. "Now tell me more about that Rom box."

"It's an out-of-whack love charm," Gaylynn replied since Dylan seemed to have lost his train of thought the moment he'd looked into Abigail's eyes. "It's been in our family for years."

"Legend has it that every other generation of the Janos family will find love literally where they look for it after opening that box," Michael inserted.

"You always do that, skip to the bottom line," Gaylynn complained.

"Because you take forever to say anything."

"You left out the heart of the story, the young Gypsy girl who fell in love with a no-account count who did not return her feelings. Desperate, the girl had a love spell cast on her behalf, but it wasn't done right. As Michael said, the first person of the opposite sex that you see after opening the charmed box was the person you'll fall in love with. I can vouch that it worked on Hunter and me."

"You had a crush on Hunter since you were thirteen," Dylan protested.

"It also worked on Brett and Michael," Gaylynn continued. "And now it's worked on you and Dylan. You were the one he saw right after opening the box."

"I told you I was attracted to Abbie the very first time I saw her," Dylan said to Gaylynn. "Before I even got the box."

"And what about your singing."

"Singing?" Michael groaned. "Oh, tell me he didn't."

Abigail immediately leapt to his defense. "Dylan has a beautiful singing voice."

"That proves it, then," Michael noted wryly. "The box is indeed magic."

"It turned Michael into a baby magnet," Brett inserted. "Before that, he was no good with little ones, but you should see him now."

"Dad told me that you two were thinking of opening a foster home."

Brett nodded.

"You'll do a great job, I'm sure."

Brett beamed. "Thanks. Your father said the key inside the box had unlocked Michael's heart."

"What key?" Dylan asked. "There was a flat rock inside the box—"

"A rock?" Michael said to Dylan. "What are you talking about? There was an intricate key inside, in silver with engraving on it. You better not have lost it!"

"You're both crazy," Gaylynn stated. "There was a beautiful old medallion inside that box."

"There's an easy way to settle this," Dylan declared. "I'll go get the box right now and show you."

They all piled into the cramped confines of the foreman's cabin, gathering around the bedside table where Dylan kept the box. Since Dylan had refused to let go of her hand—not that she wanted him to—Abigail was close enough to the box to see the intricate carving on top of it. There were four crescent moons in the left corner. On the right, a setting sun, with some kind of red stone in the center of it, was hovering over a ship whose sails were billowing in the wind. She could just make out a ridge of mountains along the horizon.

She momentarily got distracted by Dylan's lean fingers before realizing they were covering a wizard on the front of the box.

"Here, I'll show you what's inside," Dylan said.

The box was empty.

"Great," Gaylynn exclaimed. "You lost the medallion!"

"And the key," Michael said.

"I'm telling you there was a flat geode inside this thing!" Dylan maintained. "It was in here, I swear it was."

"What's this?" Abigail asked, pointing to the bottom of the box where two words were burned into the wood at the bottom.

"I don't know. I didn't see that before."

"Neither did I," Gaylynn said. "Let me think about this a minute. I read all the stuff I could about this box, and now that I think about it, nowhere did it ever say what was inside. I wonder if it's possible that we each saw what we needed to see inside of that box. Michael saw a key because he needed someone to unlock his heart. He was always too uptight," she added with a grin. "But Brett is curing him of that.

"And I . . . I saw the medallion. It was almost like a badge of honor, something that is given to reward valor. And indeed that medallion gave me strength when I needed it most. I might not have been able to save Hunter's life when he was hurt by the power saw were it not for that medallion."

"So what was the flat rock supposed to do for me?" Dylan asked.

Gaylynn frowned a minute before her eyes suddenly lit up and she snapped her fingers. "Not a rock, a stone! You're sure it was flat?"

Dylan nodded. "I'd never seen anything like it before."

"A flat stone can't roll. So I guess it means that your rolling-stone days are over."

"And what do these words mean?" Abigail asked, tracing them with her fingertips, amazed at the warmth they seemed to emanate.

"They're in Hungarian," Michael said.

"Call home and ask Dad," Dylan said, handing him the receiver of the old telephone near the bed.

"Yeah, Dad, it's Michael. No, don't put Hope on.... Hi, stinky britches. How's Daddy's little girl doing? That's great, honey. Now put your granddaddy back on the phone." Turning red, and turning his back on the rest of the family, Michael made a series of baby noises into the phone.

Abigail noted that it was all Hunter and Dylan could do not to crack up, while Brett was looking at her husband with such love in her eyes that it brought a lump to Abigail's throat.

"Dad, listen, we've got a question about the Rom box," Dylan finally said in a brisk tone of voice. "Do you know what was supposed to be in the box? I know I told you there was a key inside, but Gaylynn and Dylan found other things. That's part of the magic? Well, what about this?" Michael spelled out the two words. "What does that mean? Stop laughing and just tell me what it means.... What? I can't understand you. You haven't been into the *pálinka,* have you?... Okay, okay, then tell me what the words mean. I see. Thanks, Dad. I'll call again later. And stop laughing so hard, you'll have a fit."

"So what is it?" Gaylynn demanded. "What do the words mean?"

"Love charms."

"I can't believe we're alone at last!" Dylan noted with a sigh of relief.

"I hope your family will be comfortable up at the ranch house," Abigail said in a worried tone.

"I'm sure they will be. I'm not sure how comfortable we'll be on this narrow twin bed, though."

Abigail had given her room to Michael and Brett while Gaylynn and Hunter were sleeping on the Hide-A-Bed in the living room. Before that, Gaylynn and Abigail had

had a nice long talk about suggestions for the Lonesome Gap Lending Library, as well as Abigail autographing her most recent book for Gaylynn.

Dylan had opted to stay in the foreman's cabin, and Abigail was staying with him.

"I'm sure we can work something out about the bed," Abigail noted demurely while her smile was anything but reserved. Since she was already unbuttoning Dylan's shirt, he wasn't fooled by her tone of voice at all. Instead, he was intrigued by the promise in her blue eyes. And captivated by her smell of lily of the valley.

"I've always been a sucker for lily of the valley," he murmured, nuzzling her neck.

"I just have one thing to say to you, Dylan Janos."

"What's that?"

"Cowboy up!"

Epilogue

"Tell me I'm not crazy to be doing this," Abigail said as she nervously tugged on the lacy sleeve of her Victorian-style white wedding dress.

"You're not crazy to be doing this," Raj obediently recited.

"You're just saying that."

Raj rolled her dark brown eyes.

"Hey, how's it going in here?" Gaylynn popped her head around the door to ask.

"She's getting cold feet," Raj said.

"I am *not*," Abigail denied. "It's more like chilly big toes."

"Chilly big toes are perfectly acceptable," Gaylynn stated. "And to be expected."

"Expected?" Brett repeated, having just walked in. "Don't you mean *expecting*? Hunter told me the news about your pregnancy. I'm so happy for you!" Brett, a

natural born hugger, bestowed an exuberant one upon
Gaylynn.

"I should have told you myself, but I didn't want
to... upset you or anything," Gaylynn said.

"You didn't." At Abigail's look of confusion, Brett
quietly explained, "I can't give birth to any children of
my own, but that doesn't mean I won't have children.
We've already adopted little Hope, and Michael and I are
moving forward with out plans to open a foster home. In
fact, we just heard yesterday from our Realtor that the
large Victorian house we've had our eyes on in Du Page
County is ours. The owners accepted our bid. It's a
beautiful place, needs some fixing up, but then I'm good
at that. It's got lots of room—four bedrooms and a big
yard with an oak tree just perfect for a kid's swing. And
this wedding is going to be perfect, too," Brett added
confidently, moving closer to hug the nervously pacing
Abigail.

"Thanks, I needed that," Abigail said unsteadily. "I
just can't believe this is all really happening. Can something be too perfect? I mean, even my father likes Dylan
and he never likes anyone."

"Dylan has that effect on people," Gaylynn stated
with sisterly pride. "It's that unshakable confidence of
his."

"Tell me I'm not crazy to be doing this!" Dylan muttered as he nervously tugged on the black string bola tie
he wore beneath the collar of his crisp white shirt.

"Forget it," Michael retorted. "I like watching you
squirm and I still say you should have to wear a monkey
suit the same as me, not just the jacket." He flicked his
fingers over the tuxedo jacket Dylan wore with new
jeans.

"Ignore him," Hunter advised Dylan. "He's just teed off that he has to wear a tuxedo and you don't. Now me, I did the smart thing and eloped. Wasn't crazy enough to be best man, either."

"Cra-zee!" Hope squealed in delight as she hung on to Michael's leg. Taking a few steps backward, she ran toward him again, wrapping both arms around his leg and mashing her nose against his kneecap. "Cra-zee!" this time, her voice was a little muffled, but no less gleeful.

"I thought girls weren't allowed in here," Hunter good-naturedly grumbled.

"Relax. Hope is too young to reveal any secrets we may let drop. Isn't that right, stinky britches?"

"See-krits!" Hope squealed.

"Oh, I can tell she's the real demure, quiet type," Hunter mocked.

"Yeah, well, you'll see for yourself what it's like being a dad in what... another seven months or so?" Michael retorted.

"So, Gaylynn told you about the baby?"

"She didn't tell me," Dylan complained.

"Because you're getting married in—" tugging back the cuff of his tux, Michael checked his watch "—in ten minutes."

"Ten minutes?" Dylan paled. "Shouldn't we be in the church, waiting at the altar now?"

"Yup," Michael and Hunter said.

"Great. Great help you two are! Where's Dad?"

As if on cue, Konrad Janos entered the anteroom. "What is the delay here?" he demanded, rumpling Hope's hair with a grandfather's loving touch. "You are going to be late for your own wedding, Dylan. Michael, why is your hair all messed up like that?"

Dylan had to grin at the age-old delight of seeing his older brother discomfited as he smoothed his hair with one hand and scooped his daughter up with the other.

"It was the babies, no?" Konrad noted in resignation. "You were giving them horsie rides in the vestry again."

"He's the pied piper of babies," Dylan teased.

"And I just want to say, it couldn't have happened to a tougher guy," Hunter declared with a reassuringly mocking pat on Michael's back.

Michael's glare would have cowed lesser men, but Dylan and Hunter just laughed.

"Enough," Konrad declared with a wave of one large hand. "It is time . . . time for me to see my last born son married." He wiped away a tear.

"Hey, I thought the groom was the one who was supposed to cry," Dylan joked.

"Oh, you . . ." Konrad gave Dylan a bear hug that almost crushed his ribs. "Come on. It is time."

Abbie maintained her composure for the walk down the aisle on her father's arm. This was the wedding of her dreams; she couldn't have written a better scene. And Dylan looked incredibly dashing in his best cowboy attire. She loved him so much. She had no doubts about that.

So why was her mind a blank now? The priest was looking at her strangely, her ears were ringing, had he said something? Was this the part where she was supposed to put the ring on Dylan's hand? Or vows? Was she supposed to repeat vows now? Oh, why had she drunk that *pálinka* last night? That's why her thinking was so befuddled. The Hungarian brew was strong enough to scorch anyone's brain!

Her panic was about to spiral out of control when Dylan gently squeezed her trembling fingers and leaned over to whisper in her ear, "Cowboy up, Abbie."

Dylan's grin was contagious. So was his love. In an instant, Abigail's panic disappeared, enabling her to repeat her vows with confidence. But first she brazenly whispered to her soon-to-be husband, "I'm going to hold you to that, cowboy!"

*   *   *   *   *

Take 4 bestselling love stories FREE

Plus get a FREE surprise gift!

Special Limited-time Offer

Mail to Silhouette Reader Service™

3010 Walden Avenue
P.O. Box 1867
Buffalo, N.Y. 14240-1867

YES! Please send me 4 free Silhouette Desire® novels and my free surprise gift. Then send me 6 brand-new novels every month, which I will receive months before they appear in bookstores. Bill me at the low price of $2.90 each plus 25¢ delivery and applicable sales tax, if any.* That's the complete price and a savings of over 10% off the cover prices—quite a bargain! I understand that accepting the books and gift places me under no obligation ever to buy any books. I can always return a shipment and cancel at any time. Even if I never buy another book from Silhouette, the 4 free books and the surprise gift are mine to keep forever.

225 BPA A3UU

Name	(PLEASE PRINT)	
Address	Apt. No.	
City	State	Zip

This offer is limited to one order per household and not valid to present Silhouette Desire® subscribers. *Terms and prices are subject to change without notice.
Sales tax applicable in N.Y.

UDES-698   ©1990 Harlequin Enterprises Limited

As seen on TV!
Free Gift Offer

With a Free Gift proof-of-purchase from any Silhouette® book,
you can receive a beautiful cubic zirconia pendant.

This gorgeous marquise-shaped stone is a genuine cubic
zirconia—accented by an 18" gold tone necklace.

(Approximate retail value $19.95)

Send for yours today...
compliments of ▼ *Silhouette*®

To receive your free gift, a cubic zirconia pendant, send us one original proof-of-
purchase, photocopies not accepted, from the back of any Silhouette Romance™,
Silhouette Desire®, Silhouette Special Edition®, Silhouette Intimate Moments®
or Silhouette Yours Truly™ title available in August, September, October, November and
December at your favorite retail outlet, together with the Free Gift Certificate, plus a
check or money order for $1.65 U.S./$2.15 CAN. (do not send cash) to cover postage and
handling, payable to Silhouette Free Gift Offer. We will send you the specified gift. Allow
6 to 8 weeks for delivery. Offer good until December 31, 1996 or while quantities last.
Offer valid in the U.S. and Canada only.

Free Gift Certificate

Name: _____

Address: _____

City: _____ State/Province: _____ Zip/Postal Code: _____

Mail this certificate, one proof-of-purchase and a check or money order for postage
and handling to: SILHOUETTE FREE GIFT OFFER 1996. In the U.S.: 3010 Walden
Avenue, P.O. Box 9077, Buffalo NY 14269-9077. In Canada: P.O. Box 613, Fort Erie,
Ontario L2Z 5X3.

FREE GIFT OFFER   084-KMD
ONE PROOF-OF-PURCHASE
To collect your fabulous FREE GIFT, a cubic zirconia pendant, you must include this
original proof-of-purchase for each gift with the properly completed Free Gift Certificate.

084-KMD-R

*'Tis the season for
holiday weddings!*

This December, celebrate the holidays
with two sparkling new love stories—
only from

▼ SILHOUETTE YOURS TRULY™
™

A Nice Girl Like You
by Alexandra Sellers

Sara Diamond may be a nice girl, but that doesn't mean
she wants to be Ben Harris's ideal bride. But she might
just be able to play Ms. Wrong long enough to help this
confirmed bachelor find his true wife! That is, if she
doesn't fall in love first....

A Marry-Me Christmas
by Jo Ann Algermissen

All Catherine Jordan wanted for Christmas was some
time away from the hustle and bustle. Now she was
sharing a wilderness cabin with her infuriating opposite,
Stone Scofield! But once she stood under the mistletoe
with Stone, she was hoping for a whole lot more
this holiday....

Don't miss these exciting new books,
our gift to you this holiday season!

Look us up on-line at: http://www.romance.net

XMASYT

You're About to Become a *Privileged Woman*

Reap the rewards of fabulous free gifts and benefits with proofs-of-purchase from Silhouette and Harlequin books

Pages & Privileges™

It's our way of thanking you for buying our books at your favorite retail stores.

PROOF OF PURCHASE
Offer expires March 31, 1997

SD-PP19

Harlequin and Silhouette— the most privileged readers in the world!

For more information about Harlequin and Silhouette's PAGES & PRIVILEGES program call the Pages & Privileges Benefits Desk: 1-503-794-2499

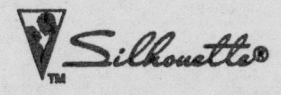

Silhouette®

SD-PP19